Marty

Marty

Eva Gibson

BETHANY HOUSE PUBLISHERS
MINNEAPOLIS, MINNESOTA 55438
A Division of Bethany Fellowship, Inc.

Marty
by Eva Gibson

Library of Congress Catalog Card Number 86–72529

ISBN 0-87123-915-9

Published by Bethany House Publishers
A Division of Bethany Fellowship, Inc.
6820 Auto Club Road, Minneapolis, Minnesota 55438

Printed in the United States of America

To Jane Gibson—
with love

EVA GIBSON, a homemaker with six children, is active in a Baptist church in Sherwood, Oregon. She is a free-lance writer whose articles have been published in several youth periodicals. She has written five other novels in the Bethany House Publishers line.

Table of Contents

Chapter 1 / The Broken Dollhouse

The old-fashioned bell on the antique store door jangled loudly as Marty shoved the door open. Just inside, she hesitated, trying to get her bearings. Her portfolio stuffed with ad clippings felt unbearably huge and awkward beneath her arm.

"What do you want?" grumbled the burly broad-shouldered man behind the counter. His beard, an interesting salt-and-pepper combination, looked at home with his brown suspenders and faded blue shirt.

His looks sure don't fit with the dainty white curtains around the store window, Marty thought. *I wish I could get his picture, that strong outdoor face contrasting with those ruffled curtains.*

Marty advanced shyly to the counter and laid her portfolio down. "I'm Marty Bauer, with the Sherwood High School yearbook staff," she explained. "I talked to you this morning."

A shadow darkened the old man's eyes. "I never talked to nobody," he said irritably.

"But—but—" Marty stammered. Nervously she pushed soft honey-colored hair away from her face. "We set up the appointment together. You said—"

The man frowned. "Don't try to put words in my mouth."

"Aren't you Mr. Norris—from the Old Town?"

The man leaned forward, propping his elbows on the counter. "Young lady, Mr. Norris works at the Old Town Tavern downtown. I'm Mr. Merwyn. This here's the Old Town Antique Shop."

"Oh, I'm sorry!" Marty's cheeks flushed crimson. "I looked it up in the phone book. But I—I must have called the wrong number!"

Something like humor glinted through the disapproval aimed at her. She smiled as she gathered confidence. "But it was you I wanted to talk to—not the tavern owner," she explained. "It's about buying ad space in the high school yearbook. I—"

"Even if you *had* talked to me on the phone, I'd have told you, 'No, I'm not interested.' " His bushy eyebrows drew together. "You might as well know, Missy. Your crowd isn't particularly welcome in my store."

"My crowd?" Marty spluttered. "I don't know what you mean."

"I guess you don't need to know." The scowl deepened, pushing the crease between his eyebrows into a furrow.

"But I do," Marty persisted. "If it's our staff—"

"It's not your staff," the old man said. "It's your age. I'm not interested in advertising in your book, girl." He changed the subject and a gentler look replaced his discouraging frown. "But if you want you can take a look around." He spread his hands wide. "Go ahead."

He dismissed her by picking up a ledger from the shelf behind him and laying it on the counter. He bent over the figures.

Marty hesitated only a moment. Her proud, stubborn self wanted to stalk out of the store with chin held high; her curious self wanted to examine the intricate design on the curved legs of the antique rocker by the window and the set of brass andirons she'd glimpsed out of the corner of her eye as she'd come through the door.

Her curiosity won. She stepped to the window, then stopped, her attention captured by a miniature hand-crafted house with wide balconies and old-fashioned pillars. It stood alone on a suspended shelf above her head, its turrets thrusting into the air.

Marty stood on tiptoe, craning her neck, peering through the curved bay windows. She glimpsed a tiny braided rug and a fireplace made of genuine tiny red bricks.

"Oh," she murmured, "it's beautiful—too perfect to be a child's dollhouse."

She spied a curved banister rising to the second floor of the dollhouse and moved closer, lifting her hand to push aside the dainty flower-trimmed curtain at the window.

"Stop!" the man behind her roared.

Marty jumped, her hand catching the edge of a pillar. "Oh! no!" she cried.

The house ignored her cry. It tipped slowly, sliding forward on the shelf.

Even as Marty raised both hands to stop its downward descent, the man was beside her, thrusting her aside. The house slammed onto the floor with a crash.

The dollhouse roof shifted forward, the pillars twisted awkwardly to one side. Marty was only vaguely aware of a grand piano thrusting through an opening in the eaves, a tiny rocking chair turned upside down on the floor.

A lump swelled in her throat as she knelt on the floor beside the broken house. "I'm sorry," she whispered, "so sorry." Her hands trembled as she reached for the miniature piano.

"Don't touch it!" Mr. Merwyn barked.

Marty's chin jerked up at his sharp command. She tried to speak but no words came.

"Get out! And don't come back. You hear?"

Marty didn't need a second order. She scrambled to her feet, her eyes burning, her cheeks scarlet with embarrassment. She bolted through the door. As it slammed shut behind her, the doorbell jangled angrily.

Marty ran down the path and onto the street, her emotions whirling. "How could I have been so clumsy?" she whispered to the October breeze touching her cheeks. Crossing the street, she added, "I should have been more careful. . . . But if he hadn't shouted so rudely at me, it wouldn't have happened in the first place," she reasoned. "It really wasn't all my fault."

She stopped at the corner and looked back. The antique store brooded alone on its tiny patch of lawn, big, square and white, its bracketed roof and small square tower rising in the center, obscuring the real personality hidden behind dainty white curtains.

Even as she watched, the heavy oak door opened. A girl with long silver blond hair slipped out. She looked in both directions, then, with head lowered, scurried across the lawn. Marty noticed an unusual bunching beneath the dark blue shirt that topped her blue jeans. Then she disappeared around the corner of the store.

Marty stared after her. Someone besides Mr. Merwyn must have witnessed her unfortunate collision with the dollhouse. But where had the girl been hiding? And why had she slipped away so stealthily? What was she hiding under her shirt?

A strange unease stirred inside Marty, and it had nothing to do with the angry man or the broken house. She heard footsteps behind her and whirled around.

Steve Lawford, editor of the school newspaper, was approaching. Would he realize she was a member of the journalism staff? Would there be any glimmer of recognition even though every other time she'd seen him he'd either been talking intently to a reporter or bent over his desk, his fingers racing over typewriter keys?

Steve hesitated a moment as he came alongside her. "Walking back to school?" he asked. "If you are, we can go together."

His smile was as warm as his thick reddish hair and the golden October afternoon. Then he looked at her, really looked at her. A slight frown erased his smile. "What's the matter?" he asked. "Trouble?"

His concern eased Marty's anger and guilt over her unfortunate encounter with Mr. Merwyn. Her answering smile turned wobbly. "I'm really all right. It's just that—" She lowered her eyes to the sidewalk, wondering how much to confide in him. "I just made somebody mad. But I didn't mean to!" She gestured toward the antique store. The story of the mistaken phone call that had resulted in her being in the store poured from her lips as they fell into step.

"Mr. Merwyn wasn't even the man I'd talked to," she said. "When I explained what I was there for, he acted so rude."

She shook her head. "Then he got mad when I accidentally knocked his precious antique dollhouse down—I don't blame him for being angry, but he didn't have to yell.

"I wish I hadn't broken it," she added regretfully. "It was beautiful—so old and perfectly detailed."

"I know Mr. Merwyn," Steve said unexpectedly. "He goes to our church."

"Your church?" Marty spluttered. "But that—that's impossible!"

A wide smile slid across Steve's face. "Why?"

"Because—just because—church people don't act like that! If they do, they shouldn't!"

The smile disappeared from Steve's eyes. "Christians are just people," he said softly, "people who need a Savior. Churches aren't supposed to be greenhouses for saints.

They're supposed to be hospitals for sinners. My dad told me that."

"Well—if that's true"—a sudden smile flitted across Marty's face—"then I guess Mr. Merwyn would fit in nicely."

Steve didn't smile. "We all do," he added thoughtfully. "But, Marty, I think you need to know. Mr. Merwyn's frightened. I heard him tell Dad that several of his prize pieces have disappeared from the store. Dad's afraid he'll end up losing everything."

"That only makes me feel worse," Marty confessed. "But what do I do?"

She looked down at her empty hands and gasped. "I left my portfolio on the counter! He's probably so angry he'll just throw it away."

She tossed her head. "But I don't care. The way I feel right now, I don't ever want to be out selling ads again. I hate that kind of work!"

"What will Mr. Hollister say?" Steve asked. "What will you say when he sends you out?"

"Maybe I'll just refuse to go," Marty said. But even as she spoke, she wondered if she really would. Mr. Hollister was advisor for both yearbook and newspaper. What Mr. Hollister said was law in the journalism department, affectionately nicknamed the J room by both yearbook and newspaper staff.

Steve touched her arm. "Wait," he said. "Mr. Merwyn knows me. I'll get your portfolio."

"Why?" Marty questioned, raising her eyebrows. "The yearbook isn't your concern."

Steve shrugged nonchalantly. "Doesn't matter. Do you want to go with me or shall I go it alone?"

"I—"

Steve slipped his camera from his shoulder and handed it to her. "Even though he's a friend I don't want him to think I'm sleuthing around after pictures. Wait here."

He turned and sprinted across the street.

Marty stared after him, nervously fingering the camera strap. She watched as he hurried up the path leading to the antique store and opened the door. Marty could imagine its angry jingle, picture the scowling man bending over the broken dollhouse.

I wonder if Steve should have waited, she mused, *given him time to calm down.*

She leaned against the light post. The afternoon dragged on, a car passed, and then another. Still no Steve. She wondered if the camera he'd left in her care belonged to him or was school equipment.

Looking up, Marty noticed the antique store door open. Steve and the old man were framed against the darkened interior. Steve nodded as the store owner's hands waved this way and that. Marty noticed her portfolio safely tucked under Steve's arm and wished she'd gone back with him. She was anxious to know what they were saying.

The old man looked her direction and Marty felt sure he saw her staring at them. She flushed and backed into the alcove created by the corner cafe's arched entryway.

Steve found her there moments later. Marty started to exchange her portfolio for Steve's camera but he shook his head. "Allow me," he said with exaggerated chivalry as he swung the portfolio up under his arm and grinned down at her.

"What happened back there?" Marty asked.

"Not much. Sorry I took so long, but he wanted to talk."

"About me?" she asked.

"Some. Of course he feels bad about the broken dollhouse. But he thinks it's fixable, so that helped. He explained more about his problem, Marty. He's losing a lot of merchandise from his shop. First an antique doll, then a set of valuable old lamps. But I assured him you had nothing to do with it—that you're an A-1 first class citizen"—he grinned at her teasingly—"even if you are upset about selling ad space."

Guilt over her attitude toward her assignment, coupled with her responsibility for breaking the dollhouse, made her cry out. "But I didn't really mean what I said! Oh, Steve, if only I hadn't knocked that dollhouse down!"

"Accidents happen," Steve reassured her. "And Marty, Mr. Merwyn did feel bad that he'd spoken roughly to you. He kept saying, 'I shouldn't have yelled at her like that.'"

"But you see, the pieces he missed disappeared right after two high-school girls were inside the store. At first he didn't pay any attention to them because teenagers aren't really much interested in antiques. They just want to look and giggle, then leave.

"But now—" Steve sighed. "He's connecting his losses with good old Sherwood High."

Remembering the furtive girl who'd vanished around the corner of the building moments after she'd left the store brought Marty to an abrupt stop. "Steve," she said, "there was a girl in a dark blue shirt who left the store after I did. She had something bunched up under her shirt."

Steve looked down at her from his towering six-foot height. "Who was she?"

"I don't know. It was right before you came. I'd run out of the store and crossed the street. Then I stopped at the corner and looked back. A blond girl I'd never seen before stepped out the door and vanished around the corner of the building. I remember wondering where she'd come from because I hadn't seen her when I was inside."

"She could have been there, though," Steve suggested thoughtfully, "and you just didn't see her."

"Yes. There were several alcoves where one could keep out of sight."

"It makes me wonder." He shifted her portfolio to his

other arm and looked at Marty intently. "A blond, huh? Like you?"

Marty touched a strand of her own honey-colored hair. "Blonder. Mine's darker than hers."

"Your coloring is unusual," he said unexpectedly. "Most blonds have blue eyes, not brown." He changed the subject back to Mr. Merwyn. "Marty, we might be able to help Mr. Merwyn. If I think up a plan, would you want to get involved?"

"I'm—not sure," she replied hesitantly. "Only a little while ago I didn't know if you'd even recognize me when I first saw you. I've seen you only when I go through the newsroom. And then you're always busy."

"But that doesn't mean I don't notice people," Steve lowered his voice, "especially the competition. You're year-book staff and you *know* what that means."

Marty laughed delightedly. "Nobody talks about it at school. But it's there, isn't it? That friendly—and sometimes not so friendly—competition between the Arrow and the yearbook staff?"

"But it doesn't have to affect us," Steve said pointedly. "What about it, Marty? Want to help me solve the Merwyn mystery?"

"Well, when you put it like that . . ." She smiled and held out her hand. "Count me in. It can't be worse than selling ad space or lining up reluctant people for boring group shots. In fact, things could get very interesting."

She was surprised by Steve's enthusiasm. "I thought you'd be like that," he said. "Why, if Mr. Merwyn is right about high school kids being the source of his problems, then maybe we can help. With me on the newspaper and you with the yearbook, there's not much going on at school that we'll miss.

"We'll be a team. A real team."

Chapter 2 / Missing Merchandise

Afterward Marty wondered why she had agreed to help Steve. At home in her room her mind was whirling in confusion.

Kicking off her tennis shoes, she sat slumped on the edge of her bed. After a while she looked up, gazing at the walls as if probing for insight.

Some of the wall decorations were pictures she'd received as a child: three brown puppies rolling on a rug, a bouquet of roses arranged in a silver vase, an artist's rendition of the house in Jesus' parable about the wise man and the foolish man. Waves boiled up around the house while the winds screamed their eternal rage.

There were more recent additions, too: a fluffy red pompom, and a red and white felt banner embossed with Sherwood High School and their Robin Hood emblem.

She leaned forward and picked up the telephone on her bedside table. After dialing, she rolled onto her stomach and waited. "Carey? Have time to talk?"

It was a silly question. Carey always had time to talk. Ever since she'd moved to Sherwood two years ago, she'd been Marty's best friend. Their houses were only three blocks apart, and from the start they'd been what their parents called "two peas in a pod."

"But of course!" Carey's voice was sparkly and alive. Marty pictured her long slender hands pushing her brown hair away from her face.

"You'll never guess who walked me back to school today. It was that good-looking, hardworking editor—Steve Lawford."

Carey's squeal made Marty's spirits rise.

"He's not stuck up at all, Carey. In fact, we've sort of decided to work on a project together."

"Marty, tell me," Carey urged. "What happened?"

Marty gave her an exact account of her afternoon in town. But even as she talked her mood dipped again. Discontent nibbled at her as she looked around her room. Why had it always been soft pink and pale blue?

Even over the telephone Carey sensed something amiss. "Marty, what's bothering you?" she asked.

"I guess I'm bored," Marty said softly—"tired of the sameness of my life, my home. That's why I wanted to be on the yearbook staff—to do something different. Except, now I'm disappointed. Selling ads isn't creative."

She turned onto her side. "I'm bored with lots of things right now, Carey."

But Carey refused to let Marty give in to self-pity. "Well, from what you say Steve's not boring," she said tartly.

"I know. But now I'm wondering. Will Steve and I really get together, or is my imagination working overtime?" Marty sat up and slipped on her tennis shoes. "Carey, I have to start supper."

She hung up and went downstairs, her dark mood clinging like a tight pair of jeans. The rough brown-skinned potatoes she took out from under the sink suited her mood. She held them under the faucet, watching the cold water splash off their surfaces. How long had she been coming in after school and peeling potatoes for the evening meal, then setting the table, tidying the living room, and talking to her school friends on the telephone? It seemed to Marty that she was stuck in an endless rut of "sameness."

Later her parents would drift in from work. Good food smells would waft through the rooms. The evening meal would be served, the TV turned on. Later there would be beds and darkness . . . another morning . . .

I need to do something different, Marty decided. *Something to break the pattern.* She thought of the pictures in her room—a conglomeration of sixteen years of living—from small child to junior high and high school.

The phone rang, jolting Marty from her reverie.

Steve's voice pushed aside her loneliness. "Marty. It's me, Steve. You'll never guess what I've discovered."

"What is it?" Marty asked breathlessly. "What happened?"

"I called Mr. Merwyn when I got home. He told me a woman from the thrift shop in Tigard had called him about 'missing merchandise.' She said, 'It's not things people need that are sliding out the back door; it's the occasional pieces that hint of antiquity—the old, old things: an old-fashioned iron, a pair of brass candlesticks.'

"Marty, shall we check out the store in Tigard in the morning?"

A stab of anticipation raced through Marty and she suspected it had little to do with digging around an old secondhand store. "I think that would be great, Steve," she said. "I'll find out from my parents if they have other plans."

Even as she said it, she knew they wouldn't. After a late breakfast, Dad would read a western, Mom would toss clothes and sheets into the washing machine.

Saturday dullness—no date, no plans—would close in around her and Marty would be glad to get out of the house. *But I wish we were going someplace besides a secondhand store.*

Something in her tone must have suggested this to him because he continued. "Afterward we could go someplace else. Any ideas?"

Her dissatisfaction with the room she'd just left rose inside her. "This afternoon I got to looking at the pictures in my room and realized how sick and tired I was of them. Steve, I don't claim to be a photographer, but sometimes I think I might have a photographer's way of seeing things. I wish we could go on a photo hunt."

"Photos, huh? Is that why you wanted to be on the yearbook staff?"

"Yes. But now that I am, well—it's not what I expected. I know you're a shutter bug, Steve. Nobody with a camera as nice as yours could be anything but. And I've heard stories in the J room."

Steve's voice warmed with enthusiasm. "You're right. Photography's been my love for a long time, ever since Dad gave me a camera when I was in junior high. How long has photography interested you?"

"A couple of years. I must have some creative potential because I have such a longing to go out and find some really neat pictures. But I don't know where to start."

"We'll do it," Steve decided quickly. "Secondhand store, lunch—then 'click' time."

"Sounds fun," Marty said.

That evening in a flurry of anticipation, Marty stripped the pictures from her wall—all except the storm-battered house. She hesitated in front of it, wondering at her reluctance. Was it because it had always made her hear the wind? Feel the cold? Or was it because it whispered a deeper truth?

She turned at a soft knock. Her mother, home from the office, stepped inside the open door.

She was a slender woman with a short well-shaped haircut that went with her dark tailored suit and the scarlet touches at wrist and throat. Everything, from her polished fingernails to her dark classic pumps, spoke of the successful American businesswoman.

Sometimes Marty wondered how her mother put up with her and Dad. Dad was so ordinary in his blue jeans and flannel shirt, contentedly tinkering with the intricate joining of pipe elbows, unplugging clogged drains on his job, or placidly repairing a broken step at home or sawing wood for the fireplace.

Marty, on the other hand, was so bumbling and unsure of herself.

Her mother glanced around the room. "For heaven's sake—what have you done to it?"

Marty shrugged her shoulders uncomfortably. "I need a change."

Lorraine Bauer's eyebrows arched into dark wings. "What do you have in mind?" Her quick, efficient mind grasped the situation and began to run with it. "I've been hoping you'd want to do something with that hodge-podge you've had so many years. How about a nice neutral background, light almond, then big splashes of color—"

Marty's words surprised even herself. "I've something in mind already, Mother." She stopped. Where were the words to describe the outdoor photographs she was just now beginning to visualize? The warm glow of autumn's gold and bronze, the honey browns, the flashes of rich reds and oranges?

"Mother, Steve—he's from school—wants me to go with him on a photo hunt.

"We just want to see if we can be creative photographers. We might get some interesting shots of a house, or a pond, or maybe an ordinary meadow."

Mrs. Bauer nodded. "There are lots of suitable subjects in the hills around Sherwood," she said vaguely. "You'll have fun."

She wandered out, leaving Marty wondering why she'd come. Marty didn't worry about it. Mother was like that, a capable business manager, but at home something of a drifter, in and out of whatever was going on.

After laying the pictures she'd removed from the wall on her dresser, Marty went to her closet and examined her clothes. Tomorrow would be special, and she wanted to look her best.

She chose a russet pullover and her favorite blue jeans, with a bright blue jacket to match the October skies. She set her camera from school beside the outfit after changing from black and white film to color.

"I'm ready for anything now," she said to no one in particular, "and I can hardly wait until morning!"

Morning finally came, bursting with sunshine and blue skies. It pushed aside the ugly residue of a bad dream lingering in the background of Marty's consciousness; a dark hallway, the sound of thunder, a crowded living room. A flash of lightning and she'd buried her face . . .

The sunshine refused to let her dark feelings linger. It flooded Marty's room with anticipation and prodded her from her bed. Instead of the russet pullover, she chose a brilliant turquoise sweater that brought out the honey-gold lights in her hair, and the flecks of green in her gold-brown eyes. She dusted a bit of make-up across her up-turned nose, tinted her lips with color and slipped the camera strap over her shoulder.

Running downstairs she noticed her father sitting beside the coffee pot, the morning paper spread before him. He looked at her approvingly as she put bread in the toaster and got out raspberry jam and butter.

"Going somewhere special, Marty?" he asked.

Marty nodded. "A photo hunt with Steve. You'll like him, Dad. He's not only the editor of our school paper, he's a camera nut besides."

They munched their toast together in comfortable comradery as Marty explained her plans for the day. She omitted the main reason for her and Steve's outing. Tracking down an old man's missing merchandise problem by searching through a secondhand store in the next town seemed a bit farfetched in light of a new day.

But was it? Seated in the front seat beside Steve in his Datsun 210, she changed her mind. Steve's eager mind was already exploring photographic possibilities. His sharp eyes took in details Marty usually paid little attention to—like the old house midway between Sherwood and Tigard. It sat poised precariously above the gravel pit on the far side of the highway beyond the onion flats.

"Someday I'd like to get a photo of that," he explained. "But it's so far away I would need a telephoto lens to do it justice."

Looking at the house with photography in mind made something stir inside Marty. Was it because of the picture in her room? The one of the house on the rock, lashed by storms, yet standing firm, no matter what?

This house was a direct contrast. "One day it's going to fall into the pit," Marty said softly. "Already the porch is hanging over nothing. If you're going to take its picture, you'd best not wait too long."

A silence fell between them. Marty wondered if Steve was thinking of the missing antiques; her own thoughts wandered back to the house on the rock. *There had been another house, the house built on sand. The rising water had shifted the foundation, the house had fallen. . .*

Standing in the dusty aisle of the Tigard thrift shop, Marty forgot the house. Steve's eager eyes took in everything; Marty could almost feel them probing the big bins stuffed with miscellany, the shelves cluttered with a strange assortment of kitchen gadgets.

He stopped beside the racks displaying old shoes and took down a pair of scuffed cowboy boots. He grinned at

Marty. "I'm starting my photo hunt now," he explained.

Pushing them casually against the wall he stood back to adjust his lens. Suddenly Marty saw what he saw: the old floor boards, the rough paneled wall, the boots removed from weary feet, shoved against the wall . . .

"Shades of the Old West," she said softly. "But how did you know? What made you think of it?"

Steve clicked the camera. He leaned forward and frowned. His lower lip caught between his teeth as he leaned one boot to a weary slant. "I guess it's the way I see things. Ever since I can remember I've kept a close eye on my world. Things, people—they fascinate me."

Marty sighed, a little envious of his enthusiasm.

Steve adjusted the camera for a horizontal shot. "Sometimes, though, I think I'd make a good detective. Except I'd probably be wanting to take a photo in a tight spot and blow the whole thing." He swung the camera across his shoulder.

Marty reached for the boots. "But I'm not like that," she said earnestly. "Is there hope for someone like me to be a photographer? Someone who isn't particularly excited about life?" Putting the boots back on the rack, she turned to face him. "Will someone who's sort of boring and uninteresting ever be able to see—really see?"

Steve leaned toward her. Marty noticed his intensely blue flashing eyes, the earnest way he drew his brows together in frowning concentration.

"You see more than you think you do, Marty." Steve gestured around the store. "But I understand what you're saying. While we're here, let's do as the proverb says, 'kill two birds with one stone.' Let's not only look for clues to relieve the misery in an old man's face, let's look for photos, too."

Even as Marty nodded, she wondered. If she couldn't seem to make it work at school, how could she make it happen in a dusty, unlikely store stuffed with used merchandise?

They separated. Steve disappeared into an alcove stuffed with TV sets and stereo parts while she lingered beside a display of colorful scarves and old wigs.

She darted a quick look around; the store was devoid of customers. Quickly she topped her honey-colored hair with a headpiece of long black curls. Smoothing the wig into place, she grimaced at her reflection in the nearby mirror.

It doesn't suit me at all, she thought, replacing it onto the foam display head. *But then, neither would the silver blond or the soft brown.*

Wandering over to the shelves loaded high with dishes and kitchen paraphernalia, she poked an exploring finger into a box of utensils. *What mood can I capture in a picture here?* she mused over the wire whips and pastry brushes.

Her imagination failed her and she turned away. She was momentarily blinded by sunlight slanting through the store's wide windows. A ray of light, caught in a cut-glass bowl on a shelf, broke into a dozen rainbows, shedding bits of color on a white cup, a dented cake pan . . .

Marty drew a quick breath. She opened her camera case.

Would she be able to capture the queen bowl showering her worn subjects with radiance? The lemon squeezer carefully held a rainbow on its curved rim, a mismatched plate cradled another on its dusty surface.

Marty focused carefully; she could see it plainly: the cut-glass bowl impartially dispensing the sun's beauty to pie pans, cake tins and ordinary mugs. She clicked, moved forward, clicked again.

The rainbows faded and the shelf was again ordinary and bent beneath a load of assorted merchandise. Marty replaced her camera in its case and examined the bowl.

Even without the glinting sun, Marty recognized its simple beauty, instinctively knew it must be valuable. Tulips marched around the bowl's surface, opening wide their blossoms. Their intricate petals were sharp against Marty's exploring fingertips.

She picked it up and turned it in her hands. An oversized tulip etched the bottom. *If only I could capture it on film.* Then memories of the overturning dollhouse flooded her thoughts. Hastily she returned the bowl to the shelf.

She went in search of Steve and found him examining an old desk at the back of the store. He looked up. "I keep forgetting what I'm here for," he said apologetically.

He caught the excitement in her eyes. "But you haven't, have you?"

Marty touched her camera gently. "I found something to photograph," she said softly. She described the queen bowl touching her subjects with tiny transforming rainbows.

"I almost felt I was observing something personal," she explained, "something not meant for me. But at the same time I wanted nothing more than to capture it on film forever. I only hope it turns out."

"I'm sure it will," he reassured her. He shut the desk drawer. "I'd like to see that bowl. It could be valuable."

"I think so, too," Marty agreed. She led the way, threading through the aisles. She stopped abruptly at the shelf that only moments before had been filled with sunshine and rainbows, then turned agonized eyes to meet the questions mirrored in Steve's.

The cut-glass bowl that had so captured her imagination was gone. The spot where it had sat only moments before was filled with an ordinary looking wooden bowl.

Chapter 3 / The Chase

"The bowl's gone!" Marty cried. "Someone's taken it!"

Marty and Steve dashed to the store window. A red convertible, its top down, pulled away from the parking lot. Two heads were silhouetted against the front window—a man's dark head behind the wheel, a girl with streaming blond hair in the seat beside him.

The girl turned and looked over her shoulder. For a brief moment her eyes met Marty's. Then the car jerked ahead, careening around the service station island between them and the highway, leaping into the traffic flow.

Steve's voice was low, filled with emotion. "Let's get out of here." His hand caught hers, drawing her through the store's wide front doors. They ran together to Steve's car.

"We'll try to follow!" Steve exclaimed.

The car doors slammed shut behind them, the engine roared. Marty bit her lip, gripping her camera with both hands. She leaned forward, her eyes probing the cars on the highway.

"I see them—I think. They're going toward Sherwood."

Steve wheeled the car around, hesitating momentarily as the caution light flashed yellow. Then they were part of the surging traffic.

The red convertible fled before them and Steve pressed harder on the gas pedal. Marty's head was spinning with all the excitement. "Oh, Steve, do you really think they've got the queen's bowl?"

The driver of a green roadster glared at them as they whizzed past. Steve and Marty ignored him. A frown creased Steve's forehead as he gripped the wheel and concentrated on manueuvering through the moving cars.

"Should we be doing this?" Marty gasped as she twisted around in her seat, looking over her shoulder.

"Don't," Steve hissed. "Keep your eye on that red convertible."

"But we're breaking the speed limit!" Marty protested.

The light flashed red.

"Oh, no," Steve groaned.

The light caught the fleeing convertible, too; Marty drew a deep breath and tried to relax the tight ball of nerves beginning to bind her stomach into a fearsome knot. Her relief was shortlived. The light turned green and they were once again weaving through heavy traffic.

It was obvious now that the driver of the convertible knew he was being followed. The car sped like a red bullet ahead of them. The space between them widened.

Marty opened her purse and took out pencil and paper. She squinted, trying to focus on the license number of the speeding car. It was no use. She could make out the letter F clearly, but then, was it an E or a B?

"I think we're going to lose them," Steve moaned. "But I'm going to keep trying."

They were well outside the Tigard city limits before they slowed. "We lost them," Steve said. "Now what?"

"Should we report it to the police?" Marty asked. "I mean, if they *did take* the glass bowl—"

"Do you think the police would believe us?" Steve shrugged. "Well, I suppose we might as well try."

They crossed the bridge spanning the Tualatin River and pulled into a small cafe a short distance down the highway. Steve came around to Marty's side and opened the door.

"Come on," he said. "There's a phone here. Besides," he grinned teasingly, "you look like you need a break."

Marty smiled wanly. She took the hand he held out to her and stepped out. "I do feel a little shaky," she confessed. "That wild ride—Steve, I'm amazed a policeman didn't see you and arrest you for speeding."

"I'd have had it coming." He turned his head and groaned. "Oh, no."

A white police car, its lights flashing, pulled into the parking lot beside them.

Steve grimaced. "Well, at least I won't have to call."

The police officer strode up to them, his face a mask of sternness. Steve dropped Marty's hand and waited. "I know I was speeding," he explained. "But there was a reason."

The story of the disappearing antique bowl and the runaway convertible poured from him as the officer examined Steve's driver's license. His questions were brief and noncommittal.

Steve gestured toward the cafe. "I was just going to phone—alert you to what's going on."

The officer returned to his car. "He's going to radio around," Steve explained to Marty. He shrugged philosophically. "Not much we can do—except pray . . ."

Marty looked at him curiously. "You mean you really do—pray, I mean?"

Steve's blue eyes flashed. "Yes. God is an important part of my life." He ran his fingers through his thick sandy hair and grinned. "Even though I did break the speed limit."

"Ah, well," Marty teased, "since churches are hospitals for sinners, both you and Mr. Merwyn can go tomorrow and get back in shape."

A bright brick red suffused Steve's face, making the

freckles sprinkling his nose look as though they were about to jump off. "That's true enough." He rubbed his hand across his forehead. "But that doesn't mean Christians have a license to sin. Sin's ugly—it puts walls between us and God."

The officer opened his car door. "I wonder what he found out," Steve muttered as he walked over to the police car. The two stood together in serious discussion, leaning against the door. *What are they saying?* Marty wondered. *And what was Steve trying to tell me? That he actually knows God as a close personal friend?*

She sat down on the front seat, her knees jutting out the open door. Was it Steve's God that made him excited about life? Marty knew it wasn't that way with her even though she believed in God and had gone to Sunday school as a small child.

"But He's never seemed real to me," she whispered suddenly. "God, are you out there somewhere? Do you care about me?"

The growing warmth of the sunshine felt good against her knees, and she reached out, gently rubbing her palms against her jeans. She jumped when she noticed Steve standing over her, smiling broadly.

"The officer called the thrift store. You're not going to believe this, Marty, but they said they never had a cut-glass bowl like you described. That they rarely, if ever, get in much of anything that's really valuable."

"But . . ." Marty sputtered. "What about what that lady told Mr. Merwyn? I—I don't understand."

"It doesn't fit together does it? But then he talked to Mr. Merwyn. He backed up my story—at least from his viewpoint." He nodded toward the police car easing into the highway traffic. "I think Officer Randall's going to check it out. He's put our speeding convertible friends on the radio. And—get this—he only gave me a warning, even though I was doing 65 right through the middle of town."

"I'm glad. But that disappearing bowl frustrates me. He probably thinks I made it up."

"Maybe. But let's not worry over it. We've done what we could. We'll let them take care of it."

The good smells of French fries and coffee mingled into an attractive aroma as they opened the cafe door. Steve sniffed appreciatively. "I guess I must be hungry."

They selected a small booth in the corner and slid into it. Steve smiled across the table at her, and Marty's stomach did a cartwheel.

His next words put her feet back on the ground. "Are you sure the bowl was really there, Marty? The lady answering the phone talked Officer Randall into believing there wasn't anything to it."

Marty bristled. "Are you saying that I made it up? That the bowl is only a figment of imagination? If you are——"

Steve reached across the table and tried to pat her hand. Marty drew back angrily, folding her hands tightly together on her lap. Pressing her lips into a pencil-thin line, she refused to look at him.

"I'm sorry, Marty," Steve apologized. "Really I am. Sometimes my mouth goes into gear before my brain does."

Marty shrugged. "It doesn't matter—I guess. After all, I can prove it with my camera. I *did* photograph that bowl, you know."

"I know you did. And I'm sorry I said what I did. After we eat we'll head for the woods—capture some of these autumn colors on film."

Marty's anger subsided as quickly as it had erupted. "I can hardly wait to finish my roll of film and get it developed. I might even take the rainbow picture to the store—show it to the lady who said the bowl hadn't been there—except I don't know her name."

Steve nodded. "We could talk to Officer Randall. He

seemed interested and asked a lot of questions.''

The waitress came to their table and Steve ordered French fries, hamburgers and tall creamy chocolate malts. The morning sun changed to midday as they leisurely sipped their malts and enjoyed each other's company.

"The sun's right overhead so we'll miss the shadows," Steve said as they went out to the car. "But it won't matter. There's a backroad not far from here with lots of fir trees. Last spring I got several good shots of trilliums, different mosses, roots growing at odd angles. I'd like to see what this season offers.''

Marty's questing eyes examined the countryside beyond the restaurant. Tall alders and maples blocked their view of the river.

"We could go to the river," she said. "I bet there are beautiful spots we could walk to.''

"There are," Steve agreed. "Shall we?''

"No," Marty changed her mind. "Let's find your backroad.''

"It's not far," Steve said.

They got into the car and crossed the highway, swinging onto a small road that jutted off at an angle. Hazel bushes thrust close to the road edge, their soft brown leaves softening the harsh angles of fences and roadsides. Slowly the countryside changed. Hazel brush gave way to vine maples, brilliant red beneath dark green fir trees. An occasional big leaf maple stood tall, its gold leaves glowing in the brilliant afternoon light.

"A car could easily disappear on this road," Marty observed thoughtfully.

Steve looked at her curiously. "You're thinking about that red convertible, aren't you?''

Marty nodded. "Are there other roads that turn off before this one? I don't recall any.''

"There are," Steve said, "but they're not backroads. If

one wanted to get lost in a hurry, he could turn off on Beef Bend Road—or into one of those trailer parks."

"But this is better," Marty mused. "It's so all alone somehow."

A wide turnoff beside a small, meandering creek welcomed them. Marty tried to wait patiently as Steve parked the car. "This is perfect, Steve." She gestured toward the colorful leaves blazing against blue sky. "Those colors are exactly right for the photos I want."

Steve swung his camera onto his shoulder. "Do you have something special planned for them?" he asked.

"I want to redo my room," Marty explained, "with soft browns, golds, even that vine maple red. I'm planning an entire wall done with photos."

They started down the road, their cameras swinging from their shoulders. Marty was overwhelmed by a sense of satisfaction, which stayed with her as she walked through the autumn woods. She had a sudden longing to reach out her hand and let Steve take it, but she shook the thought away, trying to distract herself by closely examining a vine maple.

The brilliant leaves of the tree only made it harder for Marty to calm her emotions. She was sure her cheeks reflected their hues.

Steve stopped abruptly, his hand on her shoulder. Marty froze as a colorful Chinese pheasant stepped out of the tall brown grasses woven tight with wild rose thorns and crawling blackberry vines.

Steve's movements were studied and unhurried as he lifted his camera. The camera clicked and the bird rose into the air with a whirring sound, its tail feathers arched behind him. "Ooh," Marty breathed. "Did you get it?"

"I don't know. But I think I got it as it flew." Steve shook his head. "Did you ever see more beautiful colors on a bird?"

"And the setting," Marty marveled, "his gold and red

feathers against soft brown grass, with the vine maple leaves overhead sprouting like a giant fan.''

"I might have missed it though. I had to act fast. I just hope—"

The deep blue berries clustered on a scarlet Oregon grape bush caught Marty's eye. "This is more my speed," she explained. "It doesn't move and I can take my time."

Steve went on ahead while she examined the bush from different angles and experimented with several close-up views before pushing the button. She smiled in satisfaction, nodded her head and stepped back.

Steve was nowhere to be seen, but Marty wasn't concerned. She jumped across the dry ditch alongside the road and went up a slight incline. Farther into the woods was a mossy stump and a bending vine maple branch framed against the rich dark green of a cedar tree.

She was deep in her photo quest before she realized a car was coming up the road she and Steve had just left. The soft hum of the motor sounded strangely out of place, causing her to look up. Marty parted the branches and looked out. The car's red hood glittered against the blue October sky and the gold of the big leaf maple.

Marty couldn't hold back a startled cry.

It was the convertible she and Steve had chased through town!

Chapter 4 / The House on the Cliff

The red convertible moved slowly, cautiously down the country road.

Marty peered between the leaves. Would the dark-haired man and the blond girl be its occupants? Was it really the car she and Steve had pursued through town?

Disappointment flooded her as she caught only momentary glimpses of metallic red through the autumn tinted trees. Marty almost wished that the winter storms had come early, stripping away the leaves so her view would have been unobstructed.

Marty's frustration mounted. The flashes of red disappeared as she slipped the lens cap into place, snapped the camera into its case and started back the way she'd come.

Marty heard the car slow to a stop. The convertible must have turned around in the wide turnoff where Steve had parked. The motor sounds grew loud again. It was coming back toward her.

Marty started to run. A vine maple root snagged her, propelling her to her knees. As she fell forward she shielded her camera with her arm.

Steve appeared from nowhere. Marty felt his hand on her shoulder, heard his voice full of concern, "Marty, are you all right?"

"The red convertible," she whispered, "the one we were chasing. It's coming down the road. See if you can get its license number."

Steve ignored her plea. He pulled her to her feet, watching as she dusted moss and dirt from her knees. "Are you sure you're not hurt?"

"Of course I'm sure." Marty couldn't keep the irritation from her voice. "You're wasting time," she sputtered. "Please—"

Steve shoved the creeping limb to the ground and vaulted over it. A fir stump ahead jutted into the air and he leapt onto its mossy top.

As he parted the crimson leaves on the branches of the vine maple, he let out a long, low whistle. "It's the red convertible, all right. But what is it doing here? I thought *we* were following *it*—not the other way around."

Marty tossed her hair away from her face and joined him by the stump. She followed his gaze through the forest. "I can't see."

"You're down too low. Besides, it's already gone. I only caught a quick glimpse of its backside."

"License plate?"

Steve shook his head. "No luck." He landed on the soft moss-covered ground beside her. "That was a nasty fall you took," he said softly. "I'm glad you're okay."

"Thanks, I'm glad too!"

Marty looked at the front of her bright turquoise sweater, plucking nervously at the moss clinging tenaciously to the soft material.

"Hold it," Steve said suddenly.

Marty raised startled eyes. "That stump—your sweater," he gestured at the leaves, "those leaves. Would you, Marty?"

"Would I what?"

Steve nodded to the stump. "Hop up there. I'd like to take your picture."

Marty started to protest, then shrugged. "If you really want to—"

"I do. Wildlife photography is my first love, but I like people too." He gestured toward the stump. "Sometimes I get a big yen to combine the two."

Marty grabbed an overhanging limb and hoisted herself up. The stump was rough with rotting wood, soft with lacy moss. "I wish I had a close-up lens. This moss looks like tiny ferns."

She stood up and looked in the same direction Steve had. The road curved below. She could picture the red convertible slipping into the forest and disappearing through the shielding trees.

"Now sit down," Steve urged. "Pretend you're a model."

An impish grin flashed across Marty's face, which set her tawny eyes to dancing. She struck a model's pose; leaning forward, her elbow on her crossed knee, her chin resting on her cupped hand. Steve took a picture. "Next."

Marty giggled and tossed her head. But she refused to heed the "hold that pose" command that followed. Instead, she leaped off the stump impetuously suggesting, "Let's follow the road, see where it leads."

They stumbled through the brush together, coming out only yards from the turnoff where Steve's Datsun was parked. With unspoken consent they left the car and continued their exploration on foot.

The road wound away from the shadowy forest and through a wheat field shorn of its grain, its stubble brown and harsh. Here the sun lost its autumn coolness and beat down on them relentlessly, its beams pressing warmth through Marty's sweater. Her fluffy hair curled in damp tendrils over her forehead, and she wished she'd decided to wear something lighter.

She looked at Steve. His arms, tanned from hours in the summer sun, were bare, their brownness accentuated by the light blue T-shirt he wore. He smiled at her and she noticed the tiny crinkles framing his observant eyes.

"You look ready to melt," he sympathized. "Want to go back?"

Marty shook her head. "No," she said determinedly. "I'm like the bear who went over the mountain, 'to see what he could see . . .' "

She flushed at Steve's raised eyebrows and the question mirrored in his blue eyes. "It's a silly song Dad and I sing when we're driving alone together," she explained. "It's our way of saying we want to know what's around the bend, want to see for ourselves what we'll miss if we turn back too soon."

Steve nodded approvingly. "All right! You're my kind of girl."

Marty didn't answer. His admiration disconcerted her and she sprinted ahead to hide her embarrassment, feigning eagerness to reach the shade of the tall oaks clumped together at the field's edge. They walked through the grove together, their footsteps crunching the dry grass, the bits of old bark and twigs.

"I miss the grasshoppers," Steve said suddenly. "They should be whirring into the air."

"Maybe the coming frost moved them underground," Marty surmised.

She stopped. A row of cedars barred their way, their thick weeping branches barricading the path. Steve shoved a drooping branch aside and Marty followed.

Pausing there they enjoyed the welcome shade beneath the green canopied branches. Steve undid his camera and practiced several close-up shots of various barks studded with tiny lichens.

"It's sort of disappointing," he confessed. "Last spring

the ground was covered with trilliums and yellow Johnny-jump-ups. The mosses were deep, rich shades of green."

Marty pushed on ahead. She came out on the other side of the wood abruptly and stopped, sheer surprise making her speechless.

A deep, gaping hole yawned in front of her. On the far side perched the house Steve and she had noticed on the way into Tigard.

Marty had never seen this antiquated house up close. Her eyes examined it for details that before had gone unnoticed: curved bay windows, pillars holding up a wide balcony, a round tower toward the back of the house. The balcony sagged, remnants of white paint still clung to the protected areas, and the windows were boarded up. This house, once so beautiful, was now a trembling old relic.

Marty realized the cedar trees were an extension of a hedge that must, at one time, have separated the house from the field she and Steve had just scrambled through. A path wound around the gully edge and onto the jutting peninsula where the house perched precariously near the edge. A porch ran along two sides, the front part extending over the yawning chasm.

A twig behind her snapped and Steve parted the cedar boughs. "This *is* a surprise," he said softly. "I never dreamed the house over the gravel pit was accessible. I didn't have any idea that we'd come this far."

"You said you always wanted to photograph it," Marty said. "Now's your chance."

"I know. It's far more awesome up close than I ever dreamed it would be."

They stood together, staring at the once splendid house, now suspended over the gravel pit. "It's not exactly accessible," Marty observed. "There's a *No Trespassing* sign and I think I see a notice on the door that says, *Condemned. Do Not Enter*."

Steve was readying his camera for action. "It's not quite autumn leaves—except for that big maple beside it," he said, "but—wow—this house has a story to tell. I wonder how long it's been since I first saw it and wanted to take a picture."

"It's beyond anything I imagined," Marty confessed. "I never particularly noticed the house before today. But being so close like this—"

Her head jerked as she heard a sound nearby—an odd intrusion of sound that seemed familiar yet didn't belong to the woods, the cedar trees, the house above the cliff.

The earth under her feet trembled slightly and then Marty knew. She sat down and inched herself carefully to the crevasse edge. Looking down into the gravel pit, she wasn't surprised to see a backhoe move close to the bank, its great teeth biting into the earth.

"It's a backhoe," she called to Steve, "digging out more gravel."

"I bet it won't be long before this whole house tumbles into the pit," Steve said in a quiet, matter-of-fact voice.

"You're right if they keep taking gravel away at this rate," Marty agreed. "But, oh, I do wish they wouldn't!"

Steve looked at her curiously. "Why?" he asked.

"Because—" She stopped abruptly. How could she explain the feelings the old house aroused in her? Her jumbled feelings were somehow tangled up with the picture in her room of the house on the rock. But she couldn't put it into words.

She scooted herself back a safe distance from the edge and took out her camera.

Steve wasn't satisfied with her answer. He slid his camera back in its case and leaned against an outcropping rock. His attitude invited confidences even though his gaze continued to examine the house jutting over the pit.

Marty covertly studied his profile. It was a rugged face,

as if the features had been chiseled out of rough stone similar to the rock beneath him, yet never quite polished into completion. But that wasn't right, either. When he turned to look at her, she saw that his eyes were intuitive, perceptive. There was something tender and gentle about his mouth.

"What's bothering you, Marty?" he asked softly. "It isn't just your disappointment with the yearbook, is it?"

Marty squirmed uncomfortably, looking down at her hands cupped around her camera. She shook her head.

Steve waited. Marty was aware of the sounds around them. Below them the backhoe gnawed into the bank. Overhead a flock of disturbed crows dipped and cawed.

Lifting her head, she shyly kept her eyes averted. "Do you know God, Steve? Because . . . somehow . . . I think a lot of what I'm feeling is because . . . because—"

"Go on."

Now that Marty had taken the plunge, she felt embarrassed. "Oh, it's just that—" Then she blurted it out. "He's not real to me, Steve. I talk to some people and they act like He's their best friend. It's just not that way with me."

Shame stilled her tongue. She looked him full in the face. "And then there's you. You act like you're in love with life. Is it because you love God? Or because"—she spread her hands wide—"that's just your personality?"

The words she spoke loosened her thoughts. She continued on, not waiting for an answer. "Carey—she's my best friend. She's happy just knowing God in a plain Christmas and Easter Sunday sort of way. But Steve, if God is real, then He has to make a difference every day, doesn't He?"

The pain of not knowing was biting at her. She raised troubled eyes to Steve's. "Doesn't He?"

Steve's answer was quick. "You're right, Marty. God *has* made a difference in my life—a big difference." A faraway look gathered in his eyes. "But it didn't happen right away."

"When then?" Marty demanded.

"It started when I realized that what I believed about God had to affect my behavior, or it wasn't really believing at all. It had to do with letting what I believed influence my actions."

Like the wise man who built his house on the rock, Marty thought. Was that why she was reluctant to remove the picture in her room? Why this house on the cliff affected her so deeply?

She wished she could put her tangled thoughts into words, but she couldn't, especially since she didn't even understand them herself.

She smiled somewhat sadly up at Steve. "Thanks, Steve. I guess I just needed to talk."

He grinned at her. "Talk some more," he invited. "I'll listen."

Marty shook her head. "Not now; maybe later." She nodded in the direction of the house. "Let's take some pictures. I have a picture on the wall in my room that would look great alongside this one; that is, if I could capture this house—that yawning cavity—the way I see it now."

She jumped to her feet. "Let's follow the path to the house."

Steve abandoned his laid-back position on the rock with an enthusiastic, "Let's!"

They didn't go far.

A shout rose from the cavern below. "Hey, you! You're on private property! Get out!"

Steve and Marty whirled around, staring down into the pit. The backhoe operator stood beside his machine.

He waved his arm angrily and shouted again. "It's dangerous up there! Get lost!"

"All right," Steve called. He grabbed Marty's arm, turning her around. "Come on, let's go."

They scrambled back the way they'd come. It was only

when they were safe on the other side of the cedar hedge that they realized neither of them had taken any pictures.

They looked at each other. It was Steve who put their thoughts into words, "I didn't get one shot—not one. I kept waiting to get just a bit closer for the perfect shot.

"I got nothing—absolutely nothing."

Chapter 5 / View Through A Shop Window

The next Monday Marty and her best friend, Carey, sat in the school cafeteria.

"You seem different," Carey said, looking at Marty searchingly. "What's been happening while I've been off in sunny California?"

A teasing smile played across Marty's face. "It should be *me* who's asking *you* about your weekend. Did you meet any cute boys?"

Carey looked like she wasn't quite ready to talk. Marty glanced at the French fries on her tray, picked one up, pushed it into the ketchup and waited.

"Well." Carey decided to talk now after all. "Actually, Marty, it was boring. Mom and Dad and little brother breathing down my neck. But there was this guy . . ." Her voice lowered. "I think he might try to get in touch."

She leaned forward, flicking her long brown hair with a slender hand. "He kept popping up in the dining room. And later we swam together in the hotel pool."

She sighed bleakly. "But weekend romances can be so-o-depressing. A whole weekend out of your life and you may never see him again." She lowered her voice theatrically.

"Wasted, all wasted—makeup, scheming, sleepless nights, nothing to show for it all."

She smiled suddenly, revealing the dimples in her cheeks. "Okay, Marty. What gives? I see secrets in those gorgeous eyes of yours. Is it Steve?"

Marty laughed. How like Carey, always interested in everything that touched her life no matter how drab or boring it might be.

But Steve *wasn't* boring.

"I did go with Steve Lawford on Saturday," she said softly.

"Oh," Carey squealed. "Just think, my best friend and the Arrow editor!"

"We didn't go anywhere particularly exciting," Marty exclaimed. "At least not exciting like you'd think. Except— we did sort of uncover a mystery."

The girls leaned closer together, their lunch cooling on their trays as Marty told Carey all about Steve's call on Friday, their thrift shop expedition and the wild ride through town the next day.

"You say the girl had long blond hair." Carey twisted a long strand of her own brown hair between her fingers. "Like yours?"

"No. Mine has more gold in it—brown, too. Her's was, well, flatter, almost stiff somehow."

"Bleached," Carey surmised.

"I don't know. Carey, it was our discovery of the house on the cliff that made it special. Then that man yelled at us and spoiled it all. He made us feel like a couple of dumb kids."

She took a big bite of her hamburger. After chewing for a few minutes she continued. "But what made us both so disgusted was that we totally forgot to take even one picture. All we thought about was getting out of there."

She sighed. "Carey, that house seemed unreal, yet so

beautiful. The atmosphere was right out of a gothic novel."

Carey reached for a carrot stick. "Was it strange to be close to something you'd seen only from a distance before?" she asked.

Marty nodded, noting with approval how the azure blue of Carey's blouse accentuated the warm blue of her eyes. Carey might act and sound fluttery and shallow, but she always seemed to understand what Marty was feeling.

A warm glow swelled inside her. In a way she wished she could put into words some of the deeper feelings the house on the precipice aroused in her. Perhaps when Carey came to spend the night with her they'd talk about it.

The bell rang and the girls scrambled to unload their trays. Marty jammed her books into her blue backpack and tossed it across her shoulders with a hurried, "See you in Hetterman's 'πr^2.'"

They parted, Carey to her English class, Marty to the J room.

A mingled sense of excitement and anticipation at the possibility of seeing Steve made Marty hurry as much as did her desire to be on time. Bursting through the classroom door, she received a jumbled impression of too many faces, too many voices.

But no Steve.

She shoved her pack under her spot at the large table and tried to concentrate on the photos and bits and pieces of captions in front of her.

Traci, a long, lanky girl with a nose for anything having to do with newspapers and yearbooks, slid into the seat beside her. "Shush," she warned, glaring at Marty even though Marty hadn't opened her mouth. "He's going to tell us about the photo contest."

Mr. Hollister rapped his knuckles on the desk and the room quieted slightly. Holding a magazine high, he rattled its pages ostentatiously. "Ahem."

The eager group of yearbook staffers stopped in their various activities. They looked at Mr. Hollister expectantly.

Mr. Hollister cleared his throat. "I'm posting an important notice on the bulletin board"—he waved the paper— "an announcement of a photo contest of special interest to high school seniors; the first prize, full tuition to the University of Oregon, our own Northwest's number-one school of journalism."

A soft murmur of approval rippled through the room.

"I'd like each of you to consider entering. The competition's stiff, but taking part would force you to strive for excellence."

Traci's hand waved. "Is there a theme?"

"Yes. Nostalgia, a look at yesteryears. But what they really want are photo entries with a new imaginative twist."

Marty caught her breath. *The house poised over the edge of the gravel pit—old, nostalgic . . .*

Several students crowded forward as Mr. Hollister posted the contest information on the board. But Marty waited. She had a sudden longing to talk it over with Steve. Oh, if only they could go back to the old house!

Then another thought hit her. *What if we both enter the contest . . . are in competition with one another?*

Marty squirmed in her chair. Her thoughts made it hard to concentrate on page lay-outs and captions. She bent over the table, but her real interest was thumbtacked to the bulletin board. She had to admit that the editor's desk in the adjacent room held her interest also.

The bell rang and Marty straightened. She arranged her work into a tidy pile and hurried over to the board. The heading trumpeted at her: "Nostalgia, door to our past and future."

Several sample photos were artfully arranged on the magazine page. One, a close-up of a sulky white cat wearing a silly straw hat trimmed with daffodils, captured her attention. She could almost imagine a small child of yesterday adorning her pet for an old-fashioned Easter parade.

A hand touched her shoulder. "I see you found it," Steve said. "I was hoping you'd see the poster, want to enter."

Marty looked at him searchingly. "Are you?" she asked boldly.

"Yes."

"The old house?"

"You thought of it too."

There was satisfaction in his voice and Marty lifted her chin. "You mean you wouldn't care if I tried too?" She turned to face him. "But I wouldn't, Steve. Somehow I think of the house over the gravel pit as belonging to you."

"But it doesn't," Steve said earnestly. "Oh, I know I had the desire to photograph it first, but that doesn't mean—"

"But we both can't win," Marty said softly.

"No. But, Marty, don't you see? We both see it differently. Because we do, our photographs wouldn't be alike." His sapphire eyes sparkled and a small lop-sided smile brightened his face. "Besides, I don't want to go back to the pit alone."

Delight set Marty's expressive brown eyes to dancing. "You mean we're going back, even though that man yelled at us?"

Steve nodded slowly. "I've thought a lot about it, Marty. There weren't any signs where we were that said no trespassing. And both of us have enough common sense not to go too close to the brink. So—" he raised his hand in a parting salute—"let's get together soon."

He started to leave, then turned abruptly. His voice was low, "Have you noticed anything suspicious? Anyone resembling the pair we saw in the convertible?"

Marty shook her head. "And you?"

"No," he grinned. "We'll keep in touch. The day isn't over yet."

Picking up her pack, Marty hurried to join the stream of kids pouring into the hall. Algebra, Mrs. Hetterman and Carey waited for her around the corner.

Visions of old-fashioned nostalgia, coupled with a new imaginative slant, kept pace with Marty as she detoured from her regular route home to drop her roll of film off at the Plaza drugstore.

"I wonder what the judges are really looking for," she mumbled to no one in particular. Old mingled with new would mean different things to different people. Mr. Merwyn's ideas would be much different than hers—or Steve's.

Thinking about the photography contest made Marty view her surroundings with sharpened awareness: the bright blue in a small girl's ruffled pinafore pedaling her tricycle beside her smiling mother; Mount Hood, distant but sharp against the skyline behind the town.

As she searched for photo ideas, a picture bounced into her mind; perhaps it was the small girl riding the tricycle who triggered it.

"Ah," she murmured, "a close-up of that little girl peering into Mr. Merwyn's antique dollhouse. How perfect. Today looks at yesterday."

Thinking about antique dollhouses gave her emotions a guilty tug. A vague half-remembered dream from the night before rose into her consciousness. There'd been an old man sitting in an open doorway, trying over and over to fit together the jagged edges of broken pillars. Just as they'd come together, there'd been a strange snapping noise and the pillars had popped apart like exploding popcorn.

The dream confronted her. What if Mr. Merwyn hadn't been able to repair the dollhouse? She'd be to blame.

And I didn't even tell him I was sorry, she thought. *All*

I could think of was how humiliated I felt. That and how fast I could run away.

After dropping her film off at the drugstore, she decided to swing by the Old Town Antique store and find out for herself how the dollhouse had fared. She wished Carey hadn't had an after school dental appointment. It would have been easier not to face Mr. Merwyn alone if he saw her.

The closer she got, the slower she walked. Questions pelted her. Suppose Mr. Merwyn saw her? If he did, what would she say?

"Marty!" The call came from behind her.

Marty whirled. Carey's 10-year-old sister, Sunny, and her friend hurried down the street toward her.

"Where're you going?" Sunny asked. "Can we go with you?"

Marty reached her hand toward Sunny. "Aren't you going to introduce me to your friend?"

The clear blue eyes looking up at her were Carey's own; the little frown resting momentarily between her brows, a replica of her older sister. "I'm sorry," she said, "this is Leslie. Mother said I could go to her house."

"Ah," Marty murmured. She noted Leslie's upturned nose and the light sprinkling of freckles flecking her nose and decided she liked her.

"But where are you going?" Sunny persisted. "This is Leslie's neighborhood, not ours."

Marty hesitated. "I . . . I wanted to look at something."

"What?"

Marty smiled. "If I told, you wouldn't believe it." She laughed out loud. "I wanted to look into a store window." She cocked her head to one side. "Guess what at."

Sunny and Leslie looked at her expectantly.

"A dress," Leslie hazarded.

"A boy!" Sunny exclaimed, and Marty knew she was

identifying with Carey's exclamations and groans over "Garrett," "Ryan," "Troy."

Marty shook her head. "Both wrong. You especially, Sunny. Boys don't grow in store windows."

The girls giggled.

"We give up," they chimed.

"It's a dollhouse," Marty said.

"A dollhouse," Sunny groaned skeptically. "Are you kidding?"

"Do I look too old?" Marty asked. "Actually, it's a special dollhouse—old and beautiful. You won't find it in just any store, either. I saw it last week in the Old Town Antique store. That's why I came this way."

Sunny slipped her hand into Marty's, and Leslie followed suit. As they rounded the corner the antique store came into view.

Marty stopped, the two girls clinging like burrs to her hands.

"What is it?" Sunny asked, her gentle blue eyes probing Marty's face.

Marty sighed deeply. "I have a problem," she confessed. The story of how she'd accidentally knocked the antique dollhouse to the floor poured from her. "It made me feel awful, just terrible!" she concluded. "And Mr. Merwyn was so angry all I could think about was getting out of there."

She shook her head. "Since then, I've been worried. I even dreamed about it, that it was so badly broken no one was ever able to repair it."

Sunny nodded with quiet understanding. "You'll feel a lot better when you see it."

"I know. It's just that—oh, dear, here I am being a coward again. I just hope he doesn't see me peering through his window."

The two girls looked at each other.

Leslie nodded.

Sunny grinned.

"We'll take care of it," Leslie said.

"Wait here," Sunny commanded in her most grown-up tone of voice.

The girls gave her hands a squeeze and darted across the street. Marty watched them go, a grateful smile playing across her face.

She stepped into the corner alcove where she'd stood less than a week earlier and watched a girl with long blond hair through the same heavy oak door. This time she saw the backs of two heads—one a flying blond, the other, a short brown bob—stop in front of the wide store window. They stuck close together and Marty's heart lurched. *Mr. Merwyn, don't you dare scare my little friends!*

She needn't have worried. Afternoon stillness wrapped itself around the antique shop. The door stayed tightly closed, the white curtains didn't flutter. The two small girls blended into the quiet setting.

Leslie and Sunny looked at each other and Marty caught her breath. *Sunny's profile! What a perfect model she'd be. The eager set of her shoulders, her upturned nose: today looks at yesterday—only instead of the shop window it would be the antique dollhouse.*

A car backfired, causing Sunny and Leslie to jump together off the porch. They ran down the path, across the street and into Marty's arms.

"Oh, Marty, Marty!" Sunny wailed. "We're so sorry."

Leslie tried to sound calm as she gave Marty the bad news. "We looked through the window," she said. "There's no dollhouse anywhere. It's gone."

Chapter 6 / The Upside-Down Tree

That evening Marty and Carey sat together in Marty's dining room, their open books spread on the table, tall glasses of Coke in front of them.

"Now I have two reasons for wanting to see Mr. Merwyn's antique dollhouse," Marty said, pausing to sip her Coke.

Carey looked at her curiously. "One, of course, is to put your mind at rest. The other?"

Marty leaned her elbows on the table. "The other is the contest. Carey, this afternoon when I saw Sunny looking through Mr. Merwyn's store window, I knew I had the perfect idea for my entry. Sunny sliding aside the dollhouse curtain, peering through the little window; 'Today looks at yesterday.'" She took another sip of Coke. "I first thought of a child looking inside the house when I saw a little girl with her mother downtown. That would have been good." She shook her head saying, "But you should have seen Sunny. Her profile, the intent expression on her face. She'd be perfect."

"Except right now there is no dollhouse," Carey said practically.

Marty sighed. "I know. But if there's anyway I can find out where it is"—she shut her Civic's textbook with a bang—"I'm going. I wonder if Mr. Merwyn would ever let me photograph it."

The girls said their goodbyes for the evening, and Marty went to bed.

In spite of a sudden surge of unexpected tests and an increase in homework assignments, the next week passed pleasantly enough for Marty. She welcomed the flurry of activity that kept her from worrying about the missing dollhouse.

Not that it didn't niggle at her mind when she least wanted it to. But throughout the week she'd push it behind her with a philosophical, "He's probably having fine work done on repairs." Or "The dollhouse was there all the time. The girls just didn't look in the right place."

Until today—Friday, 3:35 p.m. Marty fumbled in her purse for her house key.

She sighed bleakly at the prospect of Carey being gone with her family again. If she were lucky she'd be back Monday, bubbling about Alan and Bob and Garret and Troy—or whomever.

Steve would be the only boy she'd talk to Carey about. He'd been so busy this week that they'd only had time to briefly discuss their total lack of new information. The mystery of the red car and Mr. Merwyn's problem with his store remained unsolved.

"We'll get together this weekend," Steve had promised.

But nothing had come together. The weekend stretched before her without one interesting plan or activity to break the monotony.

Marty pushed open the door.

"Marty!"

She turned.

Steve leaned his head out the open window of his Datsun. "Want to go sleuthing?" he yelled.

A smile broke across Marty's face. She set her backpack and purse inside her house, flipped a tress of honey-gold hair over her shoulder, and ran to him across the lawn.

Steve's broad grin wiped away the week's disappointment. "Well, do you?"

"Yes. Right now?"

"You bet. I tried to find you at school but—"

"I'll leave a note for my parents," Marty explained. She looked down at her dark cords, her trim cocoa pullover. "Do I have time to change?"

"Sure." He pulled forward into the driveway. "Wear your old jeans. We're heading for the gravel pit."

"I knew it!" Marty exulted.

They smiled at each other.

"I've been wishing we could go there all week!" she said. "I have something to show you, too."

She turned and ran into the house, pausing just long enough to scoop up her backpack and purse before heading for her room. She pulled blue jeans and a dark blue T-shirt with a scooped neck from her drawer. She looked at herself in the mirror as she put them on; her hair fell in disorder around her shoulders, her lips needed a touch of color.

She picked up a lipstick, ran a comb through her hair. Then a hastily scribbled note and she was ready, her camera swinging.

Grabbing the envelope with the pictures she'd picked up at the drugstore the day before, she ran down the stairs. One hand straightened the knit band around her waist, the other adjusted the camera strap around her neck. She stopped on the bottom step, a hand suspended in midair.

Lorraine Bauer stood in the living room, frowning at her. "Where to, Marty?"

"Mother! You're home early!" Marty looked intently at her mother, noting the fine crinkles around her eyes, the tenseness framing her mouth. She felt a pang of sudden anxiety. "Are you sick?"

Mrs. Bauer shook her head. "I got a telephone call at work. Someone I haven't seen for years wanted to see me." She sighed as she ran a distracted hand through her short dark hair. "But we didn't have as much to say to one another as we thought we would. So I came home." She tilted her head. "Is that a friend of yours in our driveway?"

Confusion momentarily flooded Marty's senses. The blood rushed to her cheeks. *Why is it always this way?* she wondered. *How come I'm never comfortable about my friends when I'm with Mother?*

Aloud she said, "It's Steve Lawford. We were going to try to photograph that old house again." She handed the note she'd written to her mother. "I'll ask him to come in."

Her mother sighed audibly. "Don't bother," she said. "You're in a hurry and I have a headache."

"But you said you weren't sick," Marty protested. "I—"

"A headache isn't sick." Her mother started up the stairs. Her voice trailed after her. "Go on and have fun in the sunshine while it's here. It certainly won't last. Not in rainy Oregon. And don't get into trouble."

Marty shrugged and picked up a light blue "just in case" jacket from the hall closet. Somehow her mother's mood had dampened Marty's exuberance. Even the unseasonably warm October day failed to raise her spirits as she went out to join Steve.

Steve stood beside the passenger door. As he opened the door wide, Marty climbed in. The unaccustomed attention made her blush against her will and she squirmed uncomfortably.

Steve slid behind the wheel. "Was that your mother?" he asked curiously.

"Yes. She wasn't feeling well or I'd have asked you in."

"She's different than I imagined her," Steve commented unexpectedly. He backed the Datsun out of the driveway, turning onto the street.

"What do you mean?" Marty asked.

"For one thing her hair is dark. After I met your father I figured you must take after your mom."

Marty twisted a strand of hair around her finger. "Daddy always says my coloring is unusual, like my grandmother's. According to him, Grandma Graham had 'golden brown eyes and hair the color of the clear pale honey she favored for breakfast.' "

"Most blonds have blue eyes," Steve agreed, "not brown." He looked at her intently. "Yours are tawny."

She sighed. Discussing blonds reminded her of the girl in the car they'd followed the day they'd last driven together. She wondered if they'd ever discover her real identity.

Steve looked at her. "What's wrong? Didn't your mom want you to go?"

"It isn't that," Marty said evasively.

She didn't want to talk about her mother, but she didn't know how to sidestep into another subject. She stared out the window instead, idly examining the familiar houses on the street—her street—good old Washington hill.

But Steve wouldn't leave it alone. "Don't you and your mom get along?"

His question broke through the fragile shell Marty had erected around her feelings. Words erupted; things she hadn't even thought through yet came to the surface.

"Ever since I can remember, I've been uncomfortable around my friends when Mother's there," she confessed. "And not just my friends, other people—period.

"Not Carey. She's my best friend. She's family! But everybody else—even Mom and Dad's friends. It just doesn't make sense!"

Knotting her hand into a fist, she pressed it against her

stomach. "And neither does the hurt I feel inside. Sometimes there's a heaviness that lies there like lead." She shook her head. "There's no reason—just no reason!"

She sighed. "Ever since I can remember, I've had a dream. It's the same dream each time. Always there's a storm and I'm so afraid. I wake up and my heart's pounding."

The railroad tracks at the foot of the hill bounced sense back into her. She stopped abruptly, biting back further words.

"It's all right," Steve reassured. "If you need to talk, I'll listen."

A lump swelled up in Marty's throat. She smiled ruefully. "You said that before. But I don't know what I need. Right now I think I've said enough."

Steve didn't press her. Instead, he divided his attention between the highway and the photographs Marty spread on the seat between them.

"See," she said triumphantly. "The bowl is real. It's right there with all that kitchen clutter."

"It's there all right," Steve agreed. "But then I knew it would be."

Marty examined the photos with obvious dissatisfaction. "I'm glad I tried taking that picture even though it's a disappointment. The beauty I saw when I snapped the picture just isn't there."

She picked it up and viewed it intently. "I'm going back to that store and show it to them," she decided. "I just wish I knew which clerk it was that said the bowl was never there. This photo does prove the bowl's existence even though it looks so ordinary—flat."

"Your close-up shot of the Oregon grape branch isn't ordinary, though."

"I like that one, too," Marty agreed. "I think I'll have it enlarged for my wall. The colors are right and I like looking at it."

She gathered the photos back into their envelope and listened as Steve shared some of his own photo mishaps. He slowed as they came close to the house above the gravel pit. "Looks like the workers have gone home now," he stated with obvious satisfaction. "That'll give us freedom to explore."

A spirit of adventure gave Marty a spark of enthusiasm. It whisked her tangled feelings about her mother and her disappointment over the queen's bowl off to some remote corner of her mind. Anticipation glowed inside her, making her fingers tingle as she protectively held her camera.

They turned off on the now familiar country road and drove to the wide spot where they'd parked before. Hiking down the road together, their cameras swung from straps around their necks. This time they didn't loiter; they were too intent on reaching their destination.

The path climbed more steeply than either Marty or Steve remembered. Before going too far, they realized they'd mistaken another path for the one they'd followed before.

"Shall we go back? Find the other path?" Steve asked.

Marty shook her head. "I think this one will get us there," she said optimistically.

Steve nodded reluctantly. "The other side of the mountain?" he kidded.

Marty laughed. "That's this bear," she agreed.

They resumed their climb. The path before them mounted upward between trees that grew precipitously out of the rocky cliff. Was the house just beyond?

They were puffing a little when they came to a woody glen tucked inside a small ravine cut out of the hillside. Green springy grass covered the clearing and a quiet pool stretched just beyond, a tiny jewel reflecting blue sky, the red of vine maple and the soft brown of alders. The serene beauty of this spot left them speechless for a moment.

"Let's explore," Marty finally uttered.

Steve was already taking out his camera. "I hope I can capture the mood of this little glade."

A thin scum covered the water close to the edge. Yet the pool wasn't stagnant. As Marty moved closer, she observed a small trickle of water on the far side running into it.

A fallen alder jutted into the water, pointing a slender finger at the pool's center. Marty stepped onto it, testing it carefully. It seemed steady enough as she edged forward. Away from the bank there was no scum; the smooth water reflected her likeness perfectly. Behind her reflection she caught the blurred movement of Steve lifting his camera.

The woods were quiet, almost too quiet. A strange uneasiness rose inside her. Was someone besides Steve watching her? She slowly crept backward, carefully maintaining her balance.

Waiting for her, Steve held his hand out as she came close. She stood and jumped the few remaining feet onto the bank. His hand closed around hers.

He seemed uneasy also as he stood listening intently. His gaze, usually so steady and penetrating, scanned the trees beyond her.

His voice was soft, muted. "Well, what do you think?"

"I didn't take any pictures," Marty answered.

She looked around and shivered. "This is a lonely place," she commented quietly. "It's beautiful and yet—"

"It's a place of secrets, isn't it?"

Marty nodded. "It makes me uncomfortable."

His hand tightened on hers. "Me too. It's almost like we've walked into a place we shouldn't be."

"But there's no one here!" Marty protested.

"I know," he agreed, sounding more sure than he felt.

They skirted the ravine and silent pond without words, their hands still clinging together. Their silence as they refound the path matched the brooding quietness around them.

They were startled to suddenly find themselves at the back of the house. It was impressive, set upon a high foundation with large decorative rock embedded in the concrete. The tower thrusting skyward seemed higher than before, and Marty realized the house had three stories.

In spite of the ugly boarded windows, the chipped and fading paint, Marty loved it on sight. She let go of Steve's hand and fumbled with her camera case.

"We can't get the shot I want from here—the cliff wall, the house teetering above it," Steve observed. "We're too close."

"I know. But that illusion of yesterday—that all alone, floating-above-the-world quality. I hope I can get it."

Her frustration over the flat quality of the cut-glass bowl pictures resurfaced. Would she fail again?

"Try several angles," Steve urged. "Don't be afraid to experiment. We can go back to the other path for the long distance shot I want." Just before he disappeared around the far side of the house, he turned and shouted encouragement. "You'll get it this time!"

Marty was left alone. She walked here and there, toying with different angles, different backgrounds. Always the *condemned* and *no-trespassing* signs interfered with the mood she longed to capture. She tried several shots but the knowledge that she wasn't getting what she wanted bothered her. Finally, she turned away.

A strange looking tree topping a slight incline behind the house caught her attention. All the tree's limbs, from the tall uppermost tip to the lower branches, grew down instead of up. They trailed to the ground, thick and almost blue-black, concealing the trunk.

Marty knew that deep within there must be a hidden place, secret and shielded. She wanted to push aside those drooping branches and step into its sheltered heart.

Snapping her camera back inside the case, she hurried

down the incline. A small path from the other side met her and she followed it to the tree.

A question began to form inside her mind. The grasses surrounding the tree were thin and worn as though other feet had frequently trodden it down. Why would this be—with the house condemned and deserted? The tree would be the perfect place for a child's fort, but there were no children around here.

The house was behind her, the sheltered ravine holding the blue pool in the palm of its hand lay before her. She saw the log she'd stood on, the tops of the alders and maples.

Someone could hide inside this tree and watch both paths . . . the old house . . . the pond . . . and no one would be the wiser. Marty remembered their feelings of unrest in the clearing. *Could someone have been watching them from deep inside the upside-down tree?*

She moved forward hesitantly and parted the tree branches. A faint breeze fingered the needles, releasing their pungent scent into the air. She sniffed in appreciation and stepped inside. It was like standing inside a fragrant cone-shaped tent—or a wigwam; the dark branches shut out the sun, enclosing her in a world apart.

It took a few minutes for her eyes to grow accustomed to the shady dimness. After a while she spotted a birdnest tucked into the branches high over her head. Beneath her feet the ground was spongy with needles.

Her foot sent a small object rolling. "No," she said softly, "it can't be."

Bending, she picked up the small wooden object cradled on the thick needles. The rocking chair from the dollhouse in Mr. Merwyn's antique shop lay on her palm, the delicate hand-carved arms and rockers clearly outlined in spite of the pale, subdued light.

Chapter 7 / Mr. Merwyn and the Rocking Chair

That night as they sat together in the family room munching popcorn, a huge jigsaw puzzle spread on the table in front of them, Marty told her father about finding the rocking chair.

"The tree where I found the rocking chair was the strangest tree I'd ever seen. The limbs grew the wrong direction—made it look like it was growing upside down."

Her father nodded. "Probably a weeping tree. They've developed different kinds besides the old-fashioned willow—weeping birches, weeping cherries, weeping beech. There are even several kinds of weeping evergreens."

Marty nodded. "That must have been what this one was. The needles were dark, almost a blue-black—a perfect hiding place to watch that old house from."

She cocked her head to one side, her gaze probing the puzzle, but her mind on the events of the day. "I bet if Steve could get a photo of that house, he could sell it to a puzzle company. With that old cedar hedge and that yawning cavity beneath it—"

Her father reached for a puzzle piece of blue sky studded with branches. "I thought you were the one taking the pictures." He poked the piece into place and looked up.

"I was," Marty explained. "But my photos don't always 'say' what I'm trying to get across. Steve's do."

Their conversation returned to the miniature rocking chair. "Steve thinks I should return it to Mr. Merwyn myself," she stated.

"Why's that?"

Marty sighed. "I suspect Steve's trying to make it easy for me to apologize to him. After all, I *did* knock his house down—but I *didn't* take its furniture."

Her father's chin jerked. "They're not thinking that, are they?"

"Steve's not," Marty shrugged. "But Mr. Merwyn—I don't know."

She pursued her thought carefully. "I think Steve wants Mr. Merwyn to get to know me so he won't be so suspicious. Steve goes to his church, you know." She took a big handful of buttery popcorn. "Dad, how would you feel if I went to church Sunday? Steve asked me."

"Church, huh? That's a switch."

"What do you mean?"

"Most kids your age are trying to get out of it. Or if they're not, they're bored stiff."

A memory of Steve's blue eyes flashed before her. Steve was alive, in love with life . . . in love with Jesus Christ. "But not Steve," she said quickly; "he's not bored about anything."

"Then by all means go," her father said. Leaning back in his chair, his attention was no longer on the puzzle before them. A thoughtful look clouded his eyes. "Your mother and I used to take you to church—Sunday school, too. Do you remember?"

"Yes. I still have the Bible I had then. The picture of the house on the rock that I earned memorizing verses is on my wall, too. Dad, why did we stop going?"

Her father shook his head. "I don't know. I guess we

just let other things push it aside. Your mom went to work, you got involved in school activities—basketball, track. And I—well, maybe I have a lazy streak. It was too easy to have a leisurely breakfast on Sunday morning—read the paper—wash the car—"

He leaned forward, "Now don't get me wrong. I'm not saying we did right. If you want to go to church with Steve, go ahead. I think it's a good thing."

Her mother entered the room. "What's a good thing, Robert?"

"I just told Marty that if she wants to go to church, it's fine with me."

"With Steve? But of course. He's a nice boy." Mrs. Bauer sank into the high-backed leather chair, the long folds of her navy blue caftan nestling around her. She sighed.

"Tired, Lorraine?" her husband asked gently. He went over to the arm of her chair and sat down, one arm around her shoulders.

Marty remembered their earlier conversation at the foot of the stairs. "Does your head still ache?"

Lorraine leaned her head back against the chair rest and closed her eyes. "I had a bad day," she confessed. "A typical Murphy's law one—everything that could go wrong did go wrong."

She opened her eyes. Her brown eyes met Marty's. "Then I met—a friend—someone I've not seen for years." Her voice lowered. "The changes were hard to handle."

A faint prickle of apprehension made Marty squirm uncomfortably. Jumping to her feet, she declared, "I'll leave you two to talk it out."

She fled to her room. *Why do I always feel this way when I'm around Mom?* she wondered. *Why can't we be friends like Carey and her mom are? Like Dad and I are?*

Even though it was early she decided to go to bed. She needed a long hot shower to wash away the dust from the gravel pit, the effects of her hike through the woods. She picked up her sleep shirt and went down the hall to the bathroom.

Afterward she sat curled up like a ball on her bed—arms clasped around her crossed legs, chin resting on her knees. *The Human Expression*, a history of peoples and their cultures, lay open in front of her. But it was hard to concentrate and she found herself reading the same paragraph several times without having any idea what she'd read.

After a while she gave up, closed the book and crawled beneath the covers. She turned off the light and let images from her day march before her: the yawning cliff wall, the old house's thrusting towers, the tiny polished rocking chair.

That made her think of Steve, Mr. Merwyn—his bristling gray beard, his angry eyes . . .

She wakened to the sound of heavy winds sweeping over the countryside. Something heavy slammed against the outside of the house.

Marty sat up. As far back as she could remember she'd hated storms—wind, the elements out of control, out of *her* control. If they came in the night, she'd do the same thing, storm after storm: pull the blankets over her head and draw her knees to her chest.

Somehow storms had been part of a recurring nightmare she'd had as long as she could remember: cracking thunder, a darkened hallway, the room bursting with sudden light. People were there but she never wanted to see who they were.

But I don't have to be like this, she thought. She pushed her covers aside and padded to the window.

There was no rain yet and streetlights illuminated the trees brightly. The fir tree close to her window was pressed into thinness, the pin oak in the neighbor's yard wrenched into tortured dancing. Leaves swirled in clusters of madness, then whirled down the street.

Marty flipped on the light. There was another storm, another night. The picture on her wall drew her as it had so many times before: the house, firm on the rock, unafraid of the wild pounding waves, the racing wind, the torrents of rain.

It's all I have to hang on to, she thought miserably. But was it? Just before she and Steve had separated, he'd said something she didn't want to forget. *That hurt you feel deep inside, Marty—I don't know much about it—but God's Word is a great healer.* She'd felt concern in the quick parting touch of his hand.

Her books were neatly placed in the small bookcase close to her bed. Bending down, she pulled out the Bible she'd received so many years before. A sudden gust of wind, filled with rain, slammed against the windowpane, and Marty dove beneath the covers.

As the rain slashed the house, the wind screamed its rage at the trees and house, and Marty quaked beneath the blankets. After a while she poked her head out, the Bible still in her hand.

She tried pushing the storm aside by opening the Bible's pages. The verses printed on the picture were from Luke 6:46–49. She propped herself up on one elbow and leafed through the pages until she found them.

"Why do you call me, 'Lord, Lord,' and do not do what I say?" she read. "I will show you what he is like who comes to me and hears my words and puts them into practice.

"He is like a man building a house, who dug down deep and laid the foundation on rock. When a flood came, the torrent struck that house but could not shake it, because it was well built."

A torrent shook the house and Marty shuddered. She fought off the thoughts of walls buckling inward, windows shattering.

She continued reading, "But the one who hears my

words and does not put them into practice is like a man who built a house on the ground without a foundation. The moment the torrent struck that house, it collapsed and its destruction was complete."

The lamp cast a circle of gold light onto the pages. Then it blinked—once—twice—and the room was enveloped in darkness. Marty closed the Bible, slipping it beneath her pillow.

The rain glared, looking flinty hard and silver against the window glass, but Marty didn't see it. Once again she'd bobbed beneath her blanket. The darkness covered her; it was almost like a coccoon, shutting her inside, safe—protected.

Marty woke to a changed world, stripped of color. She stood at her window and looked out.

The storm had blown itself out in the night, but tattered bits of water-soaked clouds shrouded the town in uncertainty. Leaves that only the day before had fluttered in the breeze had either been shoved into soggy piles against trees and fences or been blown far away. Branches and debris littered the driveways and streets.

Marty spent the morning cleaning the yard between sporadic bursts of rain. She tied up the rain-drenched chrysanthemums by the fence, gathered autumn debris and stuffed it into plastic sacks.

The neighbor's white poodle, Thunder, came over to keep her company. He raced here and there, anxiously poking his nose into everything. Before the morning was over his red ribbon was bedraggled, his white coat drenched with water and spotted with dirt.

"You're messing up your paint job, Thunder," Marty murmured sympathetically. "You're going to need a bath—new ribbons."

Thunder responded by sitting on his hind legs. His brown

eyes looked at her entreatingly. He whined softly.

Marty raked the dead leaves caught behind the flower bed toward the rock-lined edge. "I know you're anxious, Thunder. But it's only because your master took the car and you wanted to go with him.

"Now I'm anxious, too. But I have a good reason." She sighed. "I'm going to church tomorrow, Thunder. I'm going with Steve—but I'm also going to take Mr. Merwyn his rocking chair.

"Thunder, I'm scared!"

Thunder didn't wait to hear her out. His master's car pulled into the driveway next door and he shot out from under the bushes like a bullet from a gun. Marty smiled after the soggy little dog. Right now he was the exact opposite of what he'd be later that day.

Marty looked for him as she and Steve walked out to his car the next morning. Thunder was in the window where she knew he'd be, looking out at her. His paws rested on the back of the couch and he resembled a fluffy white cream puff sporting new cherry red ribbons. She waved at him and his paws pranced rhythmically, his tiny body vibrating with enthusiasm.

"He looks like he's dressed for church," Steve observed. He opened the car door for Marty and she felt his approval at her own appearance. Her cheeks flushed self-consciously as she sat down and adjusted the folds of her flared gold and brown plaid skirt.

Steve slid behind the wheel. "You and that cute puppy would make a neat pair this morning."

Marty's fingers toyed with the shiny gold buttons on her new sweater. "Thunder and I are the best of friends," she confided. "This morning we're both putting our best foot forward. He has to please his owner—I need to convince Mr. Merwyn I'm an okay teenager."

"You will," Steve reassured her. "Did you bring the rocking chair?"

Marty nodded and patted her purse. As they drove to the church she and Steve mourned the passing of the bright colored leaves.

"I'm glad we went to the gravel pit when we did," Steve said. "That one shot I took with the yellow maple arching over the house, the steep, gray-brown walls rising to the house, its porch actually jutting part way over thin air." He shook his head, "The tower, the sky—I think I caught what I went after."

Marty nodded. "The bare trees will make a difference."

She looked out the window. Steve's church, soft gray and blue, lay behind a clean stretch of green lawn, the fir trees behind framing it in restful beauty. Cars crowded the parking lot at the end of the long driveway.

Marty felt a faint whispering of butterfly wings in her stomach as she got out of the Datsun. Steve seemed to sense her nervousness; his hand on her arm steadied her, giving her confidence.

She looked around eagerly. Several couples walked toward the door; a boy with bright red hair and freckles ran to meet them.

"Hey, Steve. I approve. She's great!"

Marty flushed but Steve didn't appear to be bothered. Instead, he reached out and rumpled the boy's hair. "My baby brother, Eric," he said with a good-natured smile. "Now, little brother, get lost."

Inside the front door, Steve introduced her to his parents. Marty liked them at once; Steve had Mr. Lawford's strong profile, Mrs. Lawford's blue eyes and smile.

After they exchanged greetings, Steve guided her into a big room where a number of people milled around a coffee-pot. Marty spotted Mr. Merwyn right away; his bushy gray beard stood out like a beacon.

His eyes caught Marty's; instant recognition flared in their gray depths. As he moved in her direction, apprehension rose inside her, dimming her awareness of her surroundings. She clutched her purse tightly, the lump inside of it reminding her of what she had to say.

He stopped in front of her, his legs apart, his arms folded on his chest. "So it's you, Missy." His words were framed in a statement, but Marty knew the question he asked of her.

Her words were uncertain; she didn't know how to begin. "Mr. Merwyn, I'm here mostly because I want to tell you something."

Mr. Merwyn's stare was anything but encouraging. "Well, girl—" he said abruptly. "Spit it out."

"It's about the dollhouse. I—I went by your shop. I wanted to see if it was all right."

Mr. Merwyn shrugged. "You needn't worry over that," he said gruffly. "It's not there."

"Yes—I suspected it would be gone."

Mr. Merwyn's brows drew together. "What do you mean? What are you trying to say?"

Marty fumbled with her purse. She zipped it open, laid the tiny rocking chair in the old man's outstretched hand.

"I found this rocking chair, but that doesn't mean I know where your dollhouse is," she said evenly. "Nor does it mean I took the chair, or that I would take anything else belonging to you.

"But I *am* sorry I knocked the dollhouse down and caused you so much trouble. Will you accept my apology?"

Chapter 8 / Marty's Psalm

"Where did you find this?" Mr. Merwyn asked. His long fingers carefully smoothed the polished wood of the miniature rocking chair. "I didn't know it was missing."

Steve came to Marty's rescue. "Marty and I were taking pictures of a deserted house. Marty found this underneath a nearby tree."

Mr. Merwyn shook his head in obvious bewilderment. "I can't understand that. I packaged up the entire house, including the furniture, and sent it to a friend who does that kind of repair work."

"Perhaps you missed a piece," Steve suggested. He leaned forward. "Mr. Merwyn, what's going on, anyway? You said you suspected teenage thefts, but there has to be more to it than that. I think we could help if we knew more."

Mr. Merwyn's scowl deepened. His gaze rested on Marty.

"I owe you an apology," he said gruffly. "By returning this you proved you're not involved in anything illegal."

Marty shyly nodded her head. "I'll accept your apology—if you'll accept mine."

A smile broke across the old man's face, deepening the lines around his eyes. His hand reached for Marty's. "Share and share alike," he agreed.

Marty wasn't sure why he put it in those words, but she gave him her hand gladly, felt the earnestness and integrity in his firm handshake.

"I appreciate your confidence in me," she said softly. "It means a lot."

The bell calling them to class rang loudly. The milling people emptied into the hall but Steve and Mr. Merwyn hung back.

"Shouldn't you call your friend?" Steve asked. "See if the dollhouse is really there?"

Mr. Merwyn rubbed his beard thoughtfully. "That I should," he stated, "That I should. You kids best get to class."

But Steve wasn't to be brushed off that easily. "Will you tell us what he says? The dollhouse as well as its furniture may be missing and we need to know—that is, if you really want our help."

Mr. Merwyn nodded. His words warmed Marty's heart. "I do need your help. I'll let you know right away."

"Mr. Merwyn might be a crusty old man," Steve observed as he guided Marty to their classroom, "but he's a man of his word."

He opened the door marked, *High School—Ron Wilson*.

Marty stepped inside and looked around. She knew some of the kids from school, although other faces were unfamiliar.

She liked the teacher on sight. Ron Wilson's smile communicated the same enthusiasm for life that Steve's did. His "Welcome, Marty, so glad you're here" in response to Steve's introduction seemed genuine. His lean, strong face and the intent look in his dark eyes made her feel he was truly interested in her as a person.

She leaned forward eagerly. "The Psalms are more than poetry," Mr. Wilson was saying. "Martin Luther believed them to be a school of prayer, that it was in this book we could hear how believers talk to God.

"It's in the Psalms that we find instruction in how to pour out our hearts before God. But there's more, much more. Many of the Psalms bear the title Maskil, or teaching psalm. They're written for us to learn 'how-to' handle problems of depression, fear, pain. It's from the Psalms we learn to express joy and the sheer delight of life.

"This morning we're going to do something a bit different." Mr. Wilson picked up several blank pieces of paper and a handful of pencils. "We're each going to write our own personal psalm."

A soft groan rose around the room.

"Mr. Wilson, I can't write," the girl next to Marty protested loudly. She leaned toward Marty and whispered, "He's not being fair."

Marty looked at Steve. Already he was opening his Bible to the Psalms, a slight frown creasing his forehead. He caught the intensity of her gaze and encouraged her with a flashing smile.

"There is no right or wrong way to do this assignment," Mr. Wilson explained. "It's mainly an exercise to help you learn to pour out your feelings before the Lord. There's a list of different Psalms on the blackboard you can use as models."

"Do you want to praise God for His creation power? Try Psalm 148. Need reassurance that God is on your side? Try 18. Are you in the pits? Psalm 13 is for you. Troubled with fears? distress? unrest? Look at 107.

There was a flurry of whispers; then the room quieted.

Marty looked at the white unmarked paper in front of her, then at the board. She remembered the storm in the night, the fears she always felt when the elements raged out of control.

She turned to Psalm 107:

"Others went out on the sea in ships, they were merchants on the mighty waters. They saw the works of the Lord, his wonderful deeds in the deep.

"For he spoke and stirred up a tempest that lifted high the waves. They mounted up to the heavens and went down to the depths; in their peril their courage melted away. They reeled and staggered like drunken men; they were at their wit's end."

Marty shook her head. How strange that a book written so long ago could express her own feelings of helplessness. Wonder grew inside her as she continued to read: "Then they cried out to the Lord in their trouble, and he brought them out of their distress. He stilled the storm to a whisper; the waves of the sea were hushed.

"They were glad when it grew calm, and he guided them to their desired heaven. Let them give thanks to the Lord for his unfailing love and his wonderful deeds for men."

Marty twisted the pencil between her fingers. She began to write, "Lord, I know what it's like to have courage melt away, to feel I'm at my wit's end. I know what it's like when waves pound inside me, mounting higher and higher.

"But, Lord, you say you want to still that raging, you want to bring me out of my distress. Lord, I'm crying out to you. Hush my heart. Bring me into my desired haven."

But what was that desired haven?

Marty wasn't sure. But one thing she was sure of. She would never forget this hour when God's Word became real to her.

She listened eagerly as several volunteers read their psalms, felt amazement at how differently they'd turned out. Mr. Wilson noted it too.

Something tugged inside Marty as Mr. Wilson said, "The same Word, the same Lord, yet each one of you expressed the personality, the problems, the struggles that are uniquely you."

She listened expectantly as Steve read from the psalm

he'd written: "I love you, O Lord. You are the strength of my life. You are my Rock. You never change; you're always giving me what I need. When trouble comes I can hide in you."

Why he reads it like his God really is his rock. Marty deeply felt the need to experience the security in God that Steve knew.

As she and Steve went to join the worship service, she tried to find words to express her feelings. But her thoughts were too intense. She absently fingered the paper tucked inside her Bible.

Inside the sanctuary, sitting beside Steve and his brother, Eric, she slowly absorbed the feeling of worship, became aware of the joy in the singing. Several people shared items for prayer and praise.

Surprise seized her as Mr. Merwyn stood and asked for prayer for his business. "Business is slacking off and I'm losing money every day," he explained.

"He has a married granddaughter with multiple sclerosis he's trying to help," Eric whispered, "and two little great-granddaughters."

A lump swelled in Marty's throat. Was that why Mr. Merwyn had been so abrupt and angry with her? Had fear made him lash out? *I wonder why Steve didn't tell me before?*

After the service she hurried over to where Mr. Merwyn stood. She fumbled for words, "Steve never told me about your granddaughter, Mr. Merwyn. But Eric did. It must make you feel awful—and cross sometimes too."

The old man scowled. "Pain in the heart is no excuse to act like a mad bull," he said abruptly.

Steve came up beside her. "About the dollhouse, Mr. Merwyn—"

Mr. Merwyn cut Steve off with an abrupt, "I'll call you," and turned away.

"What a character he is," Steve murmured. "Cross and crochety—but I love him just the same."

Marty looked after him, her gold-brown eyes brooding. "I wish you'd told me about his granddaughter," she said softly. "It would have helped me understand the way he acts."

"What do you mean?"

"Pain, distress, fear—they make you do funny things." A picture rose into her mind; rising waves, a storm-tossed boat, men at their wit's end, staggering in fear. "There's pain in Mr. Merwyn's eyes. And it isn't just his business failing."

She told him what Eric had whispered to her in the service. "It must be horrible to watch someone close to you hurting and not be able to do anything to help."

Steve took her arm. "You're hurting inside yourself," he said softly. "Marty, our family is planning a picnic this afternoon—probably our last of the season. Would you like to join us? Maybe we could talk."

Marty looked at him a little uncertainly. "Yes, I think so. I'll ask my parents."

Later that afternoon Marty stuffed her Bible inside her blue backpack. For some reason she wanted it with her. She had questions she wanted answered and she wanted to read more from the Psalm that had so impressed her that morning.

Changing out of the plaid skirt she put on a pair of blue jeans. She topped it with a turtleneck pullover, touched her lips with gloss and ran a comb through her hair. It cascaded behind her, looking lovely against the creamy-colored sweater as she went downstairs to join Steve.

They met his mother and father and an energetic Eric in the park. Mrs. Lawford set potato salad, fried chicken and poppy seed rolls on the picnic table. A luscious German chocolate cake followed and Marty suddenly realized how hungry she was.

"Did you bake it, Mrs. Lawford?" she asked shyly.

Mrs. Lawford nodded. "You can call me, Lucki, Marty. All my friends do. It's short for Lucibel."

They gathered at the table and Marty was aware of more than the tall oaks overhead, the arching blue sky and the good food arrayed on the table. There was a love and comradery present that she missed in her home.

"It's our custom to hold hands when we say grace," Mr. Lawford explained. Marty felt hers taken by Steve and Eric. There was a short silence, then, "Our Heavenly Father, we thank you for the beauties of your creation, for this food you've provided. We thank you for bringing Marty here to share it with us. Bless us."

A chorus of amen's echoed around the table.

Eric made a dive for the fried chicken on the far side of the table and was waylaid by Steve's masterful, "Manners, little brother. Manners."

"Ah, this is a picnic," Eric complained. "You're not fair."

Eric stopped grabbing and waited his turn. The food was delicious and Marty ate more than usual.

Afterward she helped with clean-up. Eric ran to find a garbage can, while Marty and Lucki covered the leftovers and stowed them into the picnic hamper. Steve carried it to the car and came back with jackets for Marty and his mother.

Marty took hers gratefully. The wind had risen and a faint skiff of clouds absorbed part of the warmth of the sun.

"Want to explore?" Steve asked.

Marty nodded. She picked up her backpack from under the table and they walked to the tree-covered knoll above the river.

Below them the Willamette River surged close to the banks, pulling at the overhanging willow trees. Marty found a rock and sat down. Steve sat on the grass near her feet.

"This morning gave me a new perspective, Steve," Marty said. She watched the water swirl and eddy. "I liked Mr. Wilson and I liked what he had to say about the Psalms."

"I did too. Marty, I was hoping you'd share the psalm you wrote. I watched your face—"

"I wanted to share, at least a part of me did." She reached for her backpack at her feet and undid the zipper. "I brought it with me."

She drew out her Bible, hesitated as she unfolded the paper between its pages. "Steve, I never knew before how real the God of the Bible is. Somehow writing my thoughts out in a prayer to Him helped me sort out some of my tangled thinking."

Even as she spoke she wondered why the hand holding the paper trembled. She read her psalm slowly, with feeling, then lifted her eyes to Steve's.

"Steve, just what is the desired haven? Is it heaven? Because if it is, I'm not sure I'm going there."

"But you can be sure," Steve assured her. "To be assured of heaven you need to tell Jesus you're sorry for your sins and ask Him to forgive you. The reason He died and rose again was to be the sacrifice for our sins. When you believe in Him, He'll make you His child."

"There has to be more to it than that," Marty protested. She leaned forward, pulled at the grass growing around the edges of the rock and twirled it in her hands. "The other night when the storm was howling outside my window, I read the verses about another storm and the wise man and the foolish man. It was a story Jesus told, a parable. He said that whoever—here, let me find it."

She turned the pages in her Bible. "Here it is, it says, 'Whoever hears my words and does them is like a wise man who builds his house on a rock.' But the other man—" She raised agonized eyes to meet Steve's. "How do you *do* God's words?"

Steve shrugged. "Just day by day obeying what God says in the Bible. Of course, that means you have to know what His Word is saying. The only way to find out is to read."

Marty smiled, "And heed."

"That too." He frowned and Marty sensed him struggling to find words. "You see, heeding begins with a relationship, a relationship with Jesus Christ. Marty, if you're not sure where you stand with Him, you need to make sure."

The wind moved the trees on the far side of the river. Marty and Steve watched it pattern the water into ripples and swirls as it advanced toward them.

"God's Spirit is like the wind, even though He's a real person, the same as Jesus," Steve said. "You can't see Him but He's here. It's He who will show you Jesus."

The wind shoved against the leaning willow trees, pulled at the dead fragments of leaves still tightly clinging. It pushed against the open book, fluttering the pages.

Marty shivered and closed the Bible. She put it inside her backpack and stood up.

Steve reached over and put his hand on hers. "Read the first chapter of John, Marty," he said earnestly. "It will tell you what to do."

Chapter 9 / A Flash Of Light

Read the first chapter of John, Marty. It will tell you what to do. The words Steve had spoken at the river ran through Marty's thoughts, troubling her with their intensity.

After she returned home, she went to her room. Its narrow confines stifled her. She found herself pacing from window to bed to dresser, then back again.

Read the first chapter of John, Marty. It will tell you what to do.

Marty kicked off her tennis shoes and reached for her backpack. As she started to take her Bible out she paused, looking up at the picture of the storm-beaten house on the rock. A yearning rose inside her. She wanted to go to the ledge where she could see the yawning pit and the house suspended so close to the edge.

Unzipping the backpack, she drew out her Bible. Her fingers leafed through the pages. She stopped at Luke, slipped a piece of paper between the pages and placed the Bible back inside.

She stood with quick decision. She'd go to the old house and try to recapture some of the wonder she'd felt when she'd first seen it close up and jutting over the edge of the gravel pit.

There she would read the words Steve had suggested she

read. But first she'd read again the parable Jesus told. Perhaps she could even catch some of her feelings with her camera.

Looking out the window, she saw the late afternoon light on the tall fir tree casting shadows across the lawn. Marty grabbed a bright cherry-red hooded sweat shirt and pulled it over her head. She liked the warmth of the sweatshirt. It made her feel cozy in the brisk autumn weather.

She put her camera inside the backpack and went in search of her father. She found her parents in the family room, watching a movie on TV. As she started to speak, Marty was silenced by her father's uplifted hand.

She picked up a cushion from the basket chair and sat down. Her slender fingers toyed restlessly with the pompom edging while her thoughts sought to follow the plot. She was grateful when a commercial for Goodyear tires flashed across the screen.

Her father turned to her. "What were you wanting to say, Marty?"

"Nothing much. I—I just was wondering if you'd care if I took the car over to the gravel pit. It's not far."

Mr. Bauer looked at her curiously. "That place must really fascinate you," he observed.

"I'd like to try photographing it when the shadows are long." Marty squirmed uneasily, knowing she wasn't being entirely honest. "The time would be about right—I think."

Her father reached into his pocket and tossed his keys to her. As Marty left the room she heard her mother say indulgently, "You spoil that girl, Bob. Really you do."

"And why not?" her father asked. "She's my only daughter. Next to you, my best girl."

A shiver of nervous apprehension touched Marty's heart and she began to run. Why did being reminded of her father's and mother's close relationship always make her feel edgy? like a storm rising? like thunder crashing?

She slid behind the wheel of the red Volvo and backed out of the driveway. Once she was out of town, she looked around eagerly. Sunlight slanted across the fields, and the shadows resting beneath the trees were all she had imagined they would be.

Anticipation of capturing not only the shadowed atmosphere but something deep from the pages of her Bible touched off a feeling of excitement within her. She pressed harder on the gas.

The graveled side road invited her and she slowed, marveling at the change the recent storm had wrought on the countryside. Leafless maples stretched barren arms to the skies; she could even see the stump she had posed on for Steve's picture. Now sodden leaves lumped against the base; the green mosses could barely be glimpsed beneath the leaf covering.

She parked where she and Steve had parked and hurried down the road. Sunshine highlighted the newly bared branches, enhancing the occasional solitary leaf left to dangle alone.

Marty began to run, her backpack banging against her shoulder. She was out of breath by the time she parted the cedar branches and stepped out on the peninsula across from the deserted house. The shadows were all she had anticipated. Somehow they made the gravel pit wall seem higher than ever. The recent rain had brought an intensity to the brown cliffs that she hadn't noticed before, and the new starkness of the leafless trees only made them appear more dramatic.

Marty took her camera out of its case and focused carefully. She took several horizontal shots, scowled, then turned her camera vertically.

A soft "aah" escaped her lips. The steep wall patterned with shadow accentuated the distance between the tall tower and the gravel pit floor. Marty imagined the earth beneath the house giving way—downward, downward, yesterday's memory swallowed by today.

After a while she found a comfortable seat fairly dry beneath the shelter of the cedar hedge and leaned back against the trunk, waiting for the coming twilight. She took out her Bible. Her fingers found the slip of paper she'd slid between the pages of Luke's Gospel. She read slowly, thoughtfully. The story of the foolish man and the wise man took on new meaning in the presence of the precariously placed house.

"It's going to slide into the pit one of these days," she murmured, "and great will be the fall of it."

She could imagine the earth's tremble as the old relic slid slowly forward, the roof and walls disappearing into a cloud of dust with a great roar as it plunged from the heights.

Her open Bible pressed close to her chest as she leaned forward, clasping her arms around her knees. "I'm like you are, old house," she whispered. "My life is built on an unstable foundation, not on faith in Jesus Christ. If I don't do some right kind of building . . ."

She sighed. "God, in Steve's psalm, he called you 'his Rock.' I'd like you to be my Rock, too."

Read the first chapter of John, Marty. It will tell you what to do.

Marty turned the pages of her Bible. The light faded as she read and then reread the chapter.

"In Him was life, and that life was the light of men," she whispered aloud. "I wish you were my light, Lord Jesus. Especially when it's dark and the winds blow."

She shivered, then continued reading, ". . . to all who received him, to those who believed in his name, he gave them the right to become children of God."

The words before her blurred and Marty knew it was more than just the receding light. She closed her Bible and bowed her head. "Lord, I want my life to have a strong foundation. I don't quite understand everything, but I know I believe in you and want to receive you. I want to be what the verse said—your child."

The dusk closed around her. "Jesus," she whispered. "You are so holy, so perfect. And I—I haven't always done right. But John said you are the Lamb of God, who takes away the sin of the world. I need you to forgive me, to take away my sin."

A soft breeze stirred the cedar branches above her, touched her arms with its gentle caress. Marty knew she wasn't alone. Somehow, maybe because of the peace and joy she suddenly felt, she *knew* she had become God's child.

After a while she opened her eyes and looked across at the old house. She took a surprised inward breath and sat still.

The departing sun had left a faint glow to the sky and a single star pierced the sky above the tower. Its dark lines stood out with an unreal beauty that accentuated dark corners and drew shadows into bold relief.

The cliff fell away steeply below the house, plunging Marty's gaze into inky blackness. *A place of secrets.*

A sense of mystery and loneliness grew inside her, dampening the joy she'd felt only moments before when she'd asked to become God's child. Her fingers sought her Bible and she stood.

She started to reach for her backpack. A sharp crackle of a twig made her hand freeze in midair. Then she saw the light—a quick bobbing pinpoint on the far side of the house. Another pricked the darkness and she drew in her breath sharply.

Something was certainly going on over by the house. But what? She peered through the darkness, her ears straining to pick up some sound that might explain what was happening.

"Marty."

Marty whirled. The voice was near, too near, coming from the cedar hedge.

The branch behind her swished. Then, with relief, she recognized the tall shape coming toward her.

"Steve!"

His voice was low, matching the quality of the night. "Your dad said you'd driven over. I was worried."

"Why?"

"Maybe because—well—" he gestured into the darkness. "It was over there you discovered the rocking chair. And Mr. Merwyn called me. The antique dollhouse is gone, Marty. Someone took it from the repairman's shop—"

"Wait," Marty interrupted. She pointed at the old house behind her. In a hushed but urgent voice she whispered, "There are lights moving over there, Steve!"

She turned, Steve close beside her, and looked again. The lights had disappeared. Then one reappeared and Marty was sure it was near the strange looking upside-down tree.

Steve reached for her hand and she gave it to him gladly. They watched the light bob up and down, then disappear.

"It's someone with a flashlight," Steve observed. "They're looking the place over."

"The police?"

"I think so. Or Mr. Merwyn himself. When he told me the dollhouse was missing, he also asked me to tell him exactly where you found the rocking chair. We're onto something, Marty. I'm sure of it."

Marty shivered and Steve's hand tightened over hers. The house now lay dark and silent. The darkness had an oppressive quality.

He looked down at her and by the shadowy half light Marty read anxiety in his face. "It could be someone else, too," he said meaningfully.

"You mean whoever took the dollhouse might be there? Now?"

"Yes." He hesitated. "Marty, I'm tempted to go for a closer look."

"Oh, Steve!" she exclaimed. "I wouldn't go by myself, but the two of us—"

"We could always turn back," he said uncertainly. "I'd watch out for you, Marty. Really I would."

She tugged at his hand. "Come on," she said. "Remember? I'm the bear who went over the mountain."

But Steve stood still. "Why *did* you come here?" he asked softly. He looked up at the tops of the cedar trees as he searched for words. "Surely it wasn't to find Mr. Merwyn's dollhouse?"

"No . . ." Marty hesitated. It was her turn to grope for words. When they came they rushed out in bits and pieces, a clutter of thoughts turned topsy-turvy. "It was the rock— I mean the house." She laughed. "Actually, it was you saying, 'Read the first chapter of John.' "

"And did you?"

"Yes. I have a new life now, Steve. Remember how I said I didn't know whether or not I'd go to heaven if I died? I know now."

The light on the far side of the quarry flashed on again and Marty pulled him forward. "Let's hurry," she begged. "If we don't, they may leave and we'll never know who it is. Steve—"

"What is it?"

"The light. There're two again."

For a moment the lights were close, almost blending into one. Then darkness swallowed them simultaneously.

"They're together now. Probably went behind something at the same time. Marty, let's go."

Steve took out a small flashlight, then changed his mind. He shoved it back into his pocket. "Better to surprise whoever it is—just in case."

Their feet found the narrow path edging the peninsula.

They followed it without words in single file, their footsteps muted by the sodden leaves.

They came out at the foot of the mound where the upside-down tree grew. Marty looked up intently. It thrust its top darkly into the night, casting a shadow that trembled eerily in the darkness.

Marty shuddered. *A perfect place to hide . . .*

A thumping sound from somewhere deep inside the old house jarred them to a stop. Marty's hand crept out, seeking reassurance. Steve's fingers tightened over hers. They stood together, frozen in a waiting silence.

Another sound—this one strange and somehow muffled. Marty opened her mouth, then shut it tightly as Steve laid a warning finger over his lips. Gently he uncurled her fingers, whispered, "Wait," and started to creep forward.

But Marty wasn't about to be left alone with a dark forboding tree that whispered sounds into the night. She moved forward cautiously, close at Steve's heels. As they moved nearer the old house, they heard the sound more clearly—as if something heavy was being dragged across the floor.

A door on the far side of the house slammed and Steve sprinted forward. A hidden shrub thrust branches out of the darkness and caught his foot. He sprawled onto the ground with a great thump.

In one dash, Marty was kneeling beside him. She reached out and touched his shoulder. "Are you all right?"

"Shh," he whispered.

They waited breathlessly, aware of complete quietness from both inside and outside the house. Marty inched forward. She rounded the corner of the house but saw nothing—except an open screen door, twisted askew—silently swinging on broken hinges.

She peered into the gloom, her eyes straining to catch a

flash of light. But whoever was there, or had been there, wasn't going to reveal his presence. Marty's only light was the faint glow from the departing sun and from occasional stars beginning to prick the sky.

Chapter 10 / Suspicions—Only Suspicions

Steve and Marty knelt together in the darkness.

"I think I twisted my knee when I fell," Steve groaned. "What a time to be put out of commission. Did you see anything, Marty?"

"Nothing other than a broken screen door. Whoever was inside disappeared too quickly. But what about you? What shall I do? How can I help?"

"Help me get my foot untangled from this root—or whatever it is." He shifted his position, reached into his pocket and handed her his pocket flashlight. "See if you can find out what's got me."

Marty turned the tiny beam onto the ground close to his feet. "It's an overgrown rhododendron branch," she observed, "tightly wrapped around your ankle. Do you carry a pocket knife?"

"Sure do," he grunted as he changed position.

He handed her the knife. "Let me hold the flashlight while you get me loose."

"I don't understand how it managed to lasso you so neatly!" Marty exclaimed as she sawed the blade back and forth against the hard unyielding wood. The inside of the branch shone pale in the miniature light circle. She stopped before the blade got too close to his ankle and snapped the last fragment apart with her fingers.

Steve grabbed his leg, straightening it gingerly. He groaned as his fingers probed his knee.

"Does it hurt much?" Marty asked anxiously.

"Not so bad now that it's out of that ridiculous position." He rubbed his knee gently. "Thanks, Marty."

He handed Marty his flashlight and reached for her arm, hoisting himself upright. He took a step forward, favoring the injured leg. "It's going to be all right," he assured her. "I can put my weight on it."

"But should you?" Marty worried. "What if you've broken something? Walking would make it worse."

Steve shrugged. He draped his arm around her shoulder. "Maybe if we could find something to wrap around it—give it support. But I don't know what." He peered through the darkened trees. "I'd sure like to know who we surprised moving around inside. Chances are it wasn't the police or Mr. Merwyn."

"Whoever was here wasn't up to any good, that's for sure," Marty agreed. "Steve, I have a scarf in my pack."

"Your pack? Where is it?"

Marty twisted, looking over her shoulder. "I must have set it down when we started to run."

Steve released her arm. "Go ahead and get it," he said. "But be careful. They—whoever *they* are—could still be lurking around."

Marty was grateful for the tiny circle of light that illuminated the way she'd come. It pushed aside the fearsome darkness, replacing it with a warm and comforting glow. It reminded her of what she'd read only a short while ago—John said Jesus was the true light that gave light to men. *He gives it to me, too*, she marveled. *Not just physical light but His truth, showing me who He is—shining through my darkness.*

Her bag lay in the middle of the path. She picked it up and retraced her footsteps to where Steve waited, his tall form crouched in the shadows.

His voice came out of the darkness. "Did you find it? Did you see anything?"

Marty set her backpack down. "Yes, to the first question, no, to the second."

She pulled the navy blue handkerchief she sometimes used as a headpiece out of her bag and began to wrap it around the injured knee. She tucked in the edges, then pulled his pant leg down. "How does it feel?"

"Not too good. But not too bad either."

"Are you ready to try the trail?"

"Almost. But first—Marty, you were telling me something important when those lights started flashing again. I want to know more. What happened when you read the first chapter of John?"

Marty stood still. "It was the 'light' verse that did it, Steve. That and the parable about the house on the rock. Then the place where Jesus said that anyone who believed in Him and received Him, why, then they could belong to Him.

"I asked Him to make me His child," she finished triumphantly. "It was that simple. Now I *know* I'll be with Him someday."

She was unprepared for the triumphant hug that Steve responded with. Her heart leaped inside her with a steady bump, bump. For a moment her cheek was pressed against his own.

He released her. His words were laced with feeling. "Marty, becoming God's child means you're a new creation. You know that don't you?"

"I—I think so. I don't exactly feel different. But here is something—"

"What?" he prodded.

"Just . . . just . . . I guess becoming a child of the God of the universe takes away some of the scary feelings I've always had." She looked at him earnestly, trying to see his profile against the night sky and sighed. "If they're still there, they don't seem to have the same power over me."

She smiled. "Of course, I haven't faced another storm yet—or another nightmare—but I will. When I do, I'm going to try to remember Jesus is my God and I'm His child. Shall we go now?"

They set out on the shortcut that bypassed the pond, Steve's arm slung across Marty's shoulders for support. Their progress was slow and they were both glad when they glimpsed their cars in the clearing.

Steve opened Marty's door. "I'll send someone back for mine," he said. Holding the car for support, he slowly made his way around to the other side.

Marty switched on the dome light and peered at him anxiously as he got inside. Steve heaved a great sigh and leaned back in the seat, stretching his injured leg at an angle. The smile he gave Marty was weary and she noticed whiteness around his mouth.

She took her key out of her backpack. "Let's get you home," she said as she started the car. "You don't look good."

Once she was out on the highway, her concern made her drive a little faster than she was accustomed. As they drove by the onion flats, Steve twisted around in his seat.

"Marty!" he exclaimed. "Ouch! I shouldn't have done that." He bent forward, clasping his knee.

"What is it?" Marty cried.

"I hurt. But it isn't that. The light! Marty, I'm sure I saw it flash just now."

"But that's impossible," Marty protested. "A flashlight wouldn't show up from this distance."

"I saw something," Steve insisted. "I know I did." In

his frustration, he smacked his fist hard against his palm. "If only I hadn't fallen and hurt my knee, we'd be there now. We'd know what was happening."

They lapsed into a puzzled silence as they sped toward Sherwood.

Marty sat alone in the lunchroom the next morning, waiting for Carey, her gaze eagerly searching the crowds already gathering around the soft drink machines. She wanted to tell her friend about the strange lights and Steve's accident, but she also wanted to share something more—the hour she'd spent alone with her Bible, with her God.

Carey pounced on her from behind, grabbing her shoulders. "Aha!" she exclaimed. "I sneaked up on you."

Marty jumped. "Don't do that," she spluttered. "If you ever do it again—"

Carey was unconcerned. "I tried to call you last night when I got home," she said pointedly, sliding into a chair. "You were gone."

Marty smiled. "I was out trying to solve a mystery," she said. "Guess who with?"

"Your mom said you'd gone for a drive—by *yourself.*"

"I did. But Steve found out where I was and came looking for me."

"Ooh!" Carey squealed. "Boys never come looking for me."

Marty giggled. She knew better. Carey's happy-go-lucky personality and pretty face made her sought after by more boys than Marty cared to even think about. But this time she didn't counter her comment with her usual, "Oh, Carey, you know that's not true."

Instead she said, "Steve and I are onto something really big, Carey. Except that right now I'm in it by myself." She recounted the story of the elusive lights and Steve's accident that had resulted in his spending the day at home with his leg elevated.

"This morning he called and asked me if I'd go over to the thrift store in Tigard after school and show my photos around." She opened her purse and drew out the snapshots of the bowl she'd photographed. "Dad even let me use the car today." She laid the photographs out on the table.

"They look kind of cluttered," Carey observed as she bent over them.

"That's not the point. The point is, the clerk in the shop actually told the police there'd never been a bowl like this in the store. Ever. But I have these to prove she's wrong. Would you go with me, Carey?"

Carey ignored her question. "It doesn't make sense to me. Do you really think there's a connection between the missing dollhouse and this bowl?" She tapped the photograph with her finger. "I bet the clerk took it home with her."

"And the lights you saw in that old house," she continued, tossing her long brown hair. "I don't understand how they could fit in either."

Her casual dismissal of the way Steve and Marty had put the pieces together irritated Marty. The story of her encounter with God that she'd so longed to share remained unspoken. She stood abruptly. "Well, if you'd rather not go—"

Carey stared up at her incredulously. "Oh, I didn't say I wouldn't go." She tapped impatient fingers along the table edge. "I can hardly wait."

The bell rang.

"I was supposed to have been to class early," Carey exclaimed, "and now—oh, dear!" She tore out of the lunchroom, calling over her shoulder, "I'll meet you out front, Marty. We'll go together."

"Forget it," Marty whispered. But she knew she

wouldn't. Carey might make her mad sometimes but she was still her best friend.

Marty gathered her books into a pile and headed for class. The day stretched before her—but without yesterday's anticipation. Today held no possibility of Steve appearing unexpectedly around a corner.

But he promised to call tonight, she remembered, quickening her pace.

The day's demands wrapped themselves around her: a heated debate in speech 101, a paste-up assignment to hand in to Mr. Hollister, an algebra test.

Three-ten at last. Carey waited for her at the big double doors. They fell into step together.

"Mr. Arnold is a bear," Carey complained. "I should have gotten at least a B on my paper, but wouldn't you know, The Bear gave me a C-." She looked ruefully at Marty. "How did your day go?"

"Uum, okay, I guess."

Carey lowered her voice. "I'm sorry about this morning, Marty. I hate it when I get like that—all wrapped up in me. Ugh, I'm ugly when I'm all hung up on Garret—"

Marty giggled, "and Troy, and David, and Paul, and Dale."

"You've got their names all mixed up," Carey laughed. "Oh, well, I deserved that." She sighed. "Sometimes, though, I wish I were more like you. You're my ideal—true blue, loyal—even when you're all wound up over your mystery man."

As they got into Marty's Volvo, Carey exclaimed, "Wow, with all the resources my folks have, they'd never trust me to drive to school. You're not only true blue, Marty, you're lucky as well."

They drove down the highway and Marty slowed, calling Carey's attention to the old house jutting out over the gravel pit. "So that's where you were last night!" Carey exclaimed. Her lips squeezed tight in the little secret smile Marty loved—the one given only to those close to her.

"I'd like to see it close up myself," she continued.

Marty increased her speed slightly. "Maybe we'll have time after we talk to the clerk at the thrift store. Steve asked me to find out if they were missing any large merchandise, too. Last night it sounded like someone was dragging something awfully heavy across the floor."

Carey bounced in the seat. "This is sort of an adventure for me, Marty. Did you know I've never been inside a secondhand store?"

Carey's high exuberance lasted until they actually stepped inside the wide front doors. Marty glanced at her friend. For a brief moment she saw the store as Carey must have seen it: colorful outdated ties waving from a rack, assorted shoes in various stages of usefulness lined up like worn out soldiers awaiting orders.

"Oh, Marty," Carey whispered. "If I was going to take something valuable, I surely wouldn't come here. I . . . I think you and Steve—"

"Shush," Marty warned. She marched up to the counter, her tense fingers clasping and unclasping against her brown suede purse. She put it on the counter and unzipped it, removing the envelope containing the photographs.

The woman at the cash register turned to her. "May I help you?" she asked.

In spite of her nervousness, Marty noticed the weary lines raying out from the woman's tired brown eyes. They made her feel like saying, "No. Let me help you."

Instead she drew out the photographs of the bowl. "I took a picture of this bowl several weeks ago when I was in your store. The bowl's gone now. Do you remember seeing it? No one else does."

Another clerk stepped inside the cash register island. "Mother—"

Marty's chin jerked up. She knew that voice.

"Why, Traci!" she cried. Her startled eyes noted her J room seatmate's hastily put together appearance—her blue smock, her tumbled brown hair. "I had no idea you worked here!"

Traci's lean cheeks flushed crimson. "I don't," she said. "At least not often."

The older woman's eyes bored into Marty, then moved to Carey standing self-consciously beside her. "You know my daughter?"

"We're on the yearbook staff," Marty said. "We sit at the same table."

Traci pounced on the photographs lying on the counter. "What are these?" she asked. "Why did you bring them here?"

"It's a picture I took of a bowl here in your store," Marty explained. "But now it's gone—and no one remembers seeing it. We think it could be valuable."

"Who's we?" Traci demanded. "Who wants it? Who's asking questions?"

Carey entered the conversation. "We are," she said sweetly. "We want that bowl. We know it was here—then it disappeared. But these photographs prove—"

The older woman broke in. "Are you trying to accuse us of something?" she asked. "Because, if you are, we aren't buying it. As for that bowl, I've never seen it in my life and I'm responsible for setting all the merchandise out in the store."

Traci's light gray eyes turned metallic. Their coldness repelled Marty, fanning a faint flicker of memory from somewhere in the back of her mind.

"Your pictures aren't proof of anything," Traci stated. "Anyone who wanted to could bring something into this store and take a photograph of it." She turned her back on Marty and Carey. "Why don't you just take your photos and get out of here?"

"Traci," her mother remonstrated.

She turned to Marty and Carey. "All you really have are suspicions—unproven suspicions—that tell us nothing. You may as well leave."

Marty hastily gathered up her photographs and shoved them into her purse while Carey stood by silently, her cheeks flushed with embarrassment. They hurried from the store without a backward glance.

Chapter 11 / The Stairs to Nowhere

The wide front doors of the thrift store slammed shut behind Marty and Carey.

"Boy, did I mess that one up!" Marty exclaimed.

"Traci's a witch," Carey spluttered as they rushed across the parking lot to Marty's red Volvo. "How can you stand working with her? Why, if I were you—"

Marty opened the door. "She's not what's bothering me," she groaned softly. "I don't want to go home, Carey. I can't face Steve. I hate letting him know I failed."

"You didn't," Carey said. "Traci did."

Marty continued her lamentation as she pulled into the highway traffic. "Nothing went the way I planned. I never even remembered to ask if they were missing any large pieces. I completely forgot."

"Don't punish yourself," Carey advised. "From what you say about Steve, he'll understand. It's Traci who bothers me. Marty, I think you made an enemy."

Marty sighed regretfully. "I know. I never really liked her particularly, but now—"

"Well—" Carey shrugged philosophically. "You might as well forget it. There's nothing you can do."

The girls lapsed into a troubled silence. They were almost alongside the onion flats before Carey said, "I don't

101

want to go home right now, either. I want to see that old house up close myself."

"Are you sure?" Marty asked doubtfully. "I kind of got the impression at the thrift store that you didn't much like run-down old things. This house is really dilapidated—ugly."

"I can handle it," Carey insisted. She clasped her palms together in earnest supplication, turned pleading blue eyes dancing with melodrama to Marty. "Take me to it, please."

They turned off on the side road and Carey looked around eagerly, her questing eyes searching the barren countryside.

"You have to walk," Marty said pointedly. "Are you sure you want to do this? You'll get your feet dirty."

Carey looked down at her spotless white Nike tennis shoes and her best blue jeans. "I don't care." She looked at her friend. "But what about you? Would you rather go home and change first?"

Marty shook her head. "I'm wash and wear. My blue jeans can take a lot."

She parked at the now familiar wide spot on the road and the girls got out. "There's a shortcut that takes you straight to the back of the house," Marty stated. "But it's steep."

"I'd rather go the way you and Steve did the first time," Carey giggled. "It sounds more romantic—cedar hedge, yawning old gravel pit, gothic house."

"Sorry to disappoint you," Marty said callously. "No boys this time."

Carey groaned. "Just my luck."

In spite of their inopportune encounter at the thrift store, they set out in a spirit of anticipation. Carey reminded Marty of a curious Blue Jay, as she turned her head this way and that, her blue eyes sparkling. She commented on the oak grove at the field's edge, lamented at the distance they were going, fussed over the effects of wet grass and dirt on her outfit.

All the time her bubbling enthusiasm contradicted each complaint, so Marty didn't pay much attention to her grumbling. "You asked for it," she said unsympathetically.

She wondered if Carey would catch the sense of mystery about the house, the aura of the past that so fascinated her and Steve.

Ducking beneath the overhanging branches of the cedar hedge, Marty held the branches apart. The old house, framed by cedar branches, stared back at them, its boarded windows accentuating its aloofness, reminding Marty of eyes deliberately hooded.

Marty turned to face her friend, watching as amazement surfaced in Carey's blue eyes. Her mouth opened but no words came.

A soft smile quirked Marty's lips. "Well, what do you think?" she asked.

Words laced with emotion tumbled from Carey's lips. "But, Marty," she cried, "I had no idea. It looks so silent, so—so secretive or something."

"Now do you see why both Steve and I are longing to capture it on film?"

Carey nodded humbly. "Why . . . why . . . it's like something out of a—a gothic novel, or— Ooh, wouldn't it be exciting to be standing right here when it tumbles into the pit? It's going to, you know."

"I know. Before it happens I want to be sure I have a good photograph of it. Not just any photograph, either. I hope the ones I took capture the mood—the feeling. It means more to me than just an old house teetering on the brink of disaster. It means—"

"Solving the mystery with Steve?"

"Yes. No. I mean that's important but—"

"Photo contest, huh? First place, maybe?"

"More than that. Come on, Carey. There's a neat place where I sat alone last night."

Marty stepped through the cedar branches to the other side of the hedge. The two girls stood shoulder to shoulder on the narrow path encircling the jutting peninsula. They looked into the yawning pit together; then Marty led the way to the sheltered area beneath a cedar several paces down the path.

She sat down and looked up at her friend. "Carey, I want to share something that happened last night."

"Happened?" Expectancy flared in Carey's eyes. She plopped down beside Marty on the root. "Well, out with it," she blurted. "What's up?"

Marty gestured to the house perched on the cliff. "Does that house remind you of anything?"

Carey's eyes widened. "Remind me of anything? No, nothing in particular."

The emotion Marty had experienced when she'd read the parable Jesus had told about the house built on the rock rose up inside her and almost overwhelmed her. How could she put into words the change that had come into her life because of the verses she'd read that night? How could she explain to her best friend something of what her new friendship with Jesus now meant to her?

"I didn't tell you before, Carey. But I brought my Bible with me that night. I sat right here and read the story Jesus told comparing the wise man with the foolish man."

Carey leaned forward eagerly. "It does, doesn't it?"

"Does what?" Marty wondered if Carey was even listening to her.

"It looks like that picture in your room." She gestured toward the gravel pit. "Except it's just the opposite—the house built," she giggled, "not on sand, but over a sliding wall of—of—"

"Dirt." Marty finished for her. She leaned her back

against the cedar trunk. "I read a chapter that Steve told me to read, too," she continued thoughtfully. "That was where I discovered that I could ask Jesus to make me His child. And He did!" Marty finished joyfully. "I know now that He's the foundation of my life—my reason for living."

Carey shrugged, "I don't know about that. And I really don't know what you're trying to tell me. But, Marty, I do know I want to explore that old relic up close."

A faint sense of disappointment stole through Marty. Didn't her best friend want to understand? Aloud she said, "Even with all those signs that say, 'No Trespassing,' and 'Condemned'?"

Carey leaped to her feet. "Let's hurry!" she exclaimed impetuously. "If that house is holding on to secrets, if there's a mystery, I want to know what it is. Now."

The girls scrambled single file onto the path. Marty pointed to the upside-down tree where she had found the tiny rocking chair from Mr. Merwyn's antique dollhouse. Carey's imagination was captured. She scampered up the knoll, stopping halfway up.

"Marty, did you see this?" she cried. She half turned, pointing to a willow tree extending leafy branches over the pit edge. Beneath its outstretched branches protruded a stairway that led to nowhere.

Marty's stomach did a downward swoop as she stared at it. "Whatever that once led to isn't there anymore."

Carey started to run toward it.

"Wait!" Marty exclaimed. "That's dangerous."

Carey stopped, a pout puckering her face. "Why are you always that way, Marty? 'Miss Cautious' doesn't have fun." She cocked her head to one side. "I'm glad you brought your camera. I'll pose for a photo that will smash every other entry. You wait." And Carey plunged heedlessly down the slope.

Trepidation made Marty's knees weak. "Please!" she

cried. She hurried after her friend. "You're being foolish! I don't want a photo that risks a life!"

Carey paid no attention. Her running feet were already descending the stairs to nowhere. She sat down on the bottom step and smiled up into Marty's frightened face. "Lights! Camera!"

Cold dread made Marty's fingers fumble. She barely focused before clicking the button downward. "All right, Miss Daredevil," she shouted. "The prize-winning photo has been taken."

The sound of cracking boards shot horror into Marty's heart. "Carey!" she screamed.

Carey heard the sound too. She started to scramble backward, up the stairs, as Marty made a flying dash down them. Their hands touched. The steps beneath their feet shuddered as Marty's hand caught her friend's and pulled her to safety.

The horrible sound of rending wood pierced the air as the two girls tumbled together onto solid ground. Marty lifted her head. The stairs to nowhere teetered precariously, then slowly tipped into the abyss.

Marty held her friend tight and stared into the pit. She knew she would never forget the sounds of splintering rotten wood and rolling earth as the stairs plunged downward. Nor would she soon forget the sight of broken boards and fallen earth, and the bittersweet realization that death had come close, not only to herself, but to Carey.

Carey's hand quivered under Marty's. "You saved my life," she whispered. "Oh, Marty—" She buried her face into Marty's shoulder and burst into tears. "I'm sorry," she wailed. "I never dreamed my silliness could be so dangerous."

The girls clung to one another. It was a while before Carey could look into the pit. Her face whitened.

"To think," she whispered, still staring downward, "I could have been lying there, tangled up in boards and dirt."

She shuddered. "Forgive me, Marty."

Marty stood, gently pulling her friend to her feet. She smiled tremulously. "Are your knees trembling like mine?"

Carey pulled a tissue out of her pocket and blew her nose. "Trembling isn't the word for it," she whispered. She tried to inject her old bravado. "My knees are knocking against each other. Rat-a-tat-tat, rat-a-tat—tat—tat—

"Oh, Marty," she wailed, "I want to go home."

It was a subdued Carey who followed Marty down the shortcut, past the pond, and into the car. Marty inexplicably felt the old house was glad to see them go.

That evening she telephoned Steve. She needed to talk to someone about her and Carey's near plunge into the quarry, but she hated to tell Steve about how she'd messed up at the thrift store.

Steve was shaken by her description of the plunging stairs to nowhere. "You shouldn't have gone there without me, Marty," he said, his voice heavy with disapproval. "You could have been killed and I—I'd have been responsible."

Marty gripped the phone, unexpectedly hurt. "Is that all you're worried about?" she asked in frustration. "Just that you'd feel responsible?"

"Marty, I didn't mean—I . . . I didn't intend for it to come out that way! Marty, are you there?"

"Yes," she whispered. "I'm sorry, Steve. I didn't mean to react like that either. I'm . . . I'm the one who's thoughtless. Is your knee all right?"

"It's okay. The doctor said no permanent damage was done. He said I can even walk on it as long as I keep it wrapped with an Ace bandage, which I am."

"Good. And, Steve," she confessed, "I've dreaded calling you." The story of her and Carey's visit to the thrift store poured from her. "I muffed it good. All my questions and photographs did was make Traci mad and her mother suspicious. Carey says I made an enemy."

There was a moment of silence; then Steve said, "You're forgetting something, Marty."

"What?"

"You're a member of God's family now. He's your defender, your refuge."

"*My* Rock? You called Him *your* Rock in the psalm you wrote."

"He's been that to me, that's for sure," Steve agreed. "This morning I read a Psalm where David cried to God to defend him because of his enemies. You can do that, too."

"Enemies? Do you mean Traci?"

"Not exactly. But sort of. Actually though, when I come to the places in Psalms that talk about enemies, I think about my personal enemies—Satan—my own self-will."

He sighed. "There's an ugly selfishness inside that sometimes rebels against doing what my Lord wants. Talk about battle. It helps me keep God's perspective in mind when I read those Psalms."

Their talk wandered from the Psalms to the intrigue at the store. "I talked to both Mr. Merwyn and Officer Randall today. They act like they think there's not much anyone can do. I guess it's up to us."

Frustration clawed at Marty as she thought about the dilemma facing the crabby old man and his family. After she and Steve hung up, she reviewed again her and Carey's failure to discover anything concrete at the thrift store. It was hard for her not to blame herself for her ineffectiveness.

That evening Marty sat long at the dining room table, her books open in front of her, trying to corral her thoughts. The neat tiny symbols of her algebra assignment were in direct contrast to her own chaotic thinking. She almost resented their orderly regimented advance across the page.

Her father watched TV in the den close by while her

mother finished up in the kitchen. She came into the dining room and Marty looked up, pressing her pencil tip against a puzzling equation.

A slight frown furrowed her mother's forehead. She sat down in the chair beside Marty and slipped out of her shoes, leaning back to press one foot against the other.

"Another bad day?" Marty asked.

Her mother nodded. "It's been hard lately," she admitted. For a moment her dark eyes entreated Marty and she looked like she wanted to say more. Instead she closed her eyes.

Her father came up beside her and put his arms around her, embracing both her and the chair. The familiar prickling rose up on the back of Marty's arm. She looked down at the page before her, hating herself for her uncomfortable emotions. *I hate myself for feeling this way. Oh, what is wrong with me?*

She lifted her head. A faint movement at the window behind her parents caught her attention. She leaped to her feet, consternation rising to replace the prickles.

Her father looked at her in alarm. He straightened, his arms dropping from around her mother. "What is it?" he asked.

"I . . . but . . . no, it couldn't be."

"What couldn't be?" he demanded.

Marty gestured toward the window. "For a moment I thought I saw a face looking in. But it must have been my imagination. There's no one there."

Her gaze went to her mother as she said the words. For a moment she was sure she saw something besides fear surface in her mother's eyes. Was it guilt?

Her father shoved the sliding glass door open. "Who's there?" he shouted. He stepped outside onto the patio.

"Honey!" her mother exclaimed, jumping to her feet.

She started to follow her husband but his voice stopped her. "There's no one here."

She took a deep breath. "Thank God," she whispered. "That's all I need." For a moment her dark eyes met Marty's. Marty felt the wall between them, sensed her mother could have said something more but didn't.

Marty slipped out of the room.

That night Marty's dream came again. Only this time there was no storm. There was a man with Traci's metallic eyes. She stared into them and then—yawning emptiness, a darkness, and she was falling . . . falling . . . falling . . .

A scream trapped inside her chest exploded, jerking her awake. A cold sweat covered her body and she knew there had been more to the dream. The man had been in their living room. Had her parents been there too? She shuddered and tried to shake off the dream.

It was no use. She lay very still. The vague realization that perhaps the dream held the key to her fears nagged at her. *If I could just reach out, somehow turn the key*. She gathered all her courage and for the first time since she'd had the dream, tried to remember details, feelings.

She saw her own small self standing in the room's open doorway, tightly clutching a Raggedy Ann doll. She saw the windows behind the shadowy dream figures flash with light, heard a blast of thunder. She'd pressed her face into her doll's soft body . . .

But darkness was everywhere, and a great trembling . . . Further memory eluded her.

Marty turned onto her side, drew her knees close to her chest. She didn't want to be afraid of nightmares, storms, of her own past. If only she could remember.

The darkness pressed in on her. After a while she pushed her dream thoughts aside, replacing them with reality. Pictures crowded into her mind. Traci and her mother behind

the cash register. Carey beside her on the trail. Then the
stairs to nowhere swinging out over emptiness . . . falling
. . . falling . . . falling.

It was a long time before she slept.

Chapter 12 / Missing Clue

The moment Marty stepped into the journalism room, she felt the animosity in Traci's glaring look.

She drew in a sharp breath. Her fingers tightened around the backpack straps. A cry, unbidden, almost unthought, swept into her mind. *Oh, God, my Rock, my Refuge. . .*

She lifted her chin and looked Traci in the eye without flinching. Traci was first to avert her eyes.

Marty walked over and set her pack on the floor beside Traci. She sat down and viewed the layout Traci had already spread on the table.

"Well, what do you think?" Traci demanded. Her voice dripped coldness but Marty chose to ignore it.

"You've balanced it well," she said. "I don't know that I can improve on it."

Traci sniffed audibly. Marty opened her textbook and began to examine the suggested layout section. She was glad when Mr. Hollister came in and began to lecture them on the different styles of yearbooks produced by different high schools and colleges in the Northwest. Afterward he invited them to look at the books themselves.

Marty didn't need a second invitation. She muttered a quick "excuse me" and hurried to the display table, glad to be out of close proximity to the girl she'd never cared for, but now thoroughly distrusted.

Mr. Hollister moved to her side as she opened a book to its advertising section. A jolly smiling hamburger looked out at them, encouraging them to bring their families to the Denver Plaza for "lunch with the pro's."

"I need you to sell ad space this week, Marty," Mr. Hollister said. "We're running short on sponsors."

A protest rose to Marty's lips. "Oh, please," she whispered. "I—I can't."

"You did a good job before," Mr. Hollister encouraged. "You will again. He handed her a page of tightly spaced columns. "Traci put this list together. You'll be responsible to contact the unmarked names."

Mr. Hollister turned away. Marty stared down in dismay at the neat typewritten list of business and telephone numbers lying across the happy hamburger face.

She looked across the room, caught the snide smile lurking at the corners of Traci's mouth. She was sure she saw animosity glitter in her eyes and her stomach plummeted. She looked away and tried concentrating on the intricately drawn roses adorning the sign proclaiming, *Ye Old Mill Flower Shoppe*.

She was glad when the bell rang and Traci disappeared out the door. She closed the yearbook she was examining, picked up the typewritten list Mr. Hollister had left, and went back to the table to claim her belongings. On the way out, she detoured inside the editor's alcove in the adjourning room.

Steve was hunched over a well-marked manuscript, gripping a pencil in his hand. His books and papers were strewn in disorderly fashion across his desk. His red hair was touseled as though he'd been running nervous fingers through it.

Marty hesitated, reluctant to claim his attention. She started to turn away.

"Marty!"

She whirled around.

Steve's eyes bored into hers. "What is it?" he asked. "Why are you leaving without saying anything?"

"I guess I thought you were too busy," she confessed.

A smile touched his lips. "But I'm never to busy for my partner," he said gently. He pushed the manuscript aside. "What happened, Marty? You look upset."

Marty laid the page Mr. Hollister had given her in front of him. "Mr. Hollister wants me to contact these businesses," she said slowly. "But that isn't what's bothering me most. It's Traci."

Steve picked up the list. "What does Traci have to do with this?"

"It's the way she looks at me, Steve. Carey said I made an enemy but I had no idea—"

"Looks won't hurt you," Steve said.

Marty lifted her chin. Her eyebrows quirked into a question and almost without realizing it, she drew back.

"I didn't mean that," Steve tried to take back his unsympathetic comment. He bent over the page Marty had set before him.

"Traci gave Mr. Hollister that list," Marty explained. "She was watching when he gave it to me."

She shivered. "The look in her eyes—her smile. I don't trust her, Steve. She's trying to get even with me because I questioned her and her mother about the missing bowl."

Steve frowned. "That could be. But Marty, you can't prove it."

An unexplainable fear gave Marty goose bumps on her arms. She picked up the paper resolutely. "I shouldn't be bothering you with my problems, Steve. I'll go now. See you later."

He nodded. "I'll meet you at the sign after school." A smile replaced the look of consternation that had spread across his face. "I have something to show you—later. Something special."

His excitement distracted Marty from her dread. She smiled. "You got your photos of the old house developed, didn't you?"

"Yes. I think you'll be impressed."

The ringing tardy bell called Marty to her next class. *I'll be late,* she thought, *but this once doesn't matter. I wonder why talking with Steve always makes me feel better?*

After the last class Marty waited beside the concrete sign marking the school entrance. Her classmates streamed around her, but it was several moments before she saw Carey coming her way. Her eager waves and greetings were strangely absent.

"What's wrong, Carey?" Marty asked, as her subdued friend came up beside her. "Did our escapade yesterday knock all the fun out of you?"

Carey nodded. "I even had trouble sleeping last night," she said in a low, troubled voice. "I kept thinking how I could have been lying at the bottom of that gravel pit instead of in my bed. And it was my stupidity, my sheer stupidity, my wanting to be in the limelight that did it."

She began twisting a long strand of her hair into a slender rope around her finger, then continued. "That was bad enough, but then I almost pulled you down with me. I'm sorry, Marty. So sorry."

"You said that before," Marty chided. "There's nothing to do now but just—" she shrugged, "put it aside and go forward."

She spotted Steve in the crowd and waved. "We're over here." She noticed the portfolio tucked under his arm as he separated himself from his classmates, eager to see the photos he'd taken.

He took her arm. "Let's get out of this mob—go to Guido's where we can talk."

Marty looked questioningly at Carey and noted the frown creasing her forehead.

"You go on ahead, Marty," Carey said. "I have to meet my little sister anyway."

"But we'd rather have you with us," Marty urged.

Steve nodded. "There's always room for one more."

But Carey shook her head obstinately. "I have to meet Sunny."

Marty looked after her as she slipped away through the crowd, then forgot her as she concentrated on the fun of being with Steve.

Once they were at Guido's, Steve selected a large table by the big window and set his portfolio down. "Coke?" he asked and Marty nodded.

He set the frosty drinks in the middle of the table and reached for the portfolio, drawing out a large sheaf of black and white eight-by-ten blow-ups. "Shut your eyes," he commanded.

Obediently Marty shut her eyes.

"Now open."

Marty opened her eyes and leaned forward. A soft "o-oh" came from her lips.

The photos Steve had spread out on the table revealed the house above the gravel pit in all its ancient splendor. The tower thrusting skyward looked taller than it did in real life; the boarded windows resembled eyelids, hiding secrets. There was no doubt that the old relic on the cliff had a definite "you are there" appeal. It leaned over the yawning cavity, ready to plummet downward, yet at the same time somehow seeming to mourn time's passage.

"Mother said it made her long for the good old days," Steve said. His finger drew her attention to the distant highway. "They're both here: nostalgia—past and present."

"Exactly what the contest wants. Steve, these photos are

good, really good." She looked up. "How are you going to choose which one to enter?"

He smiled. "I was hoping you'd help me. I showed these to Mr. Hollister before I left school today. He asked me to make a display to encourage others." He cocked his head to one side and arched his left eyebrow, "Like you."

"Don't worry about me," Marty replied confidently. "I'm going to enter. I'm not sure what, but I'm going to do it. Something in me—"

"Need me to develop anything for you in the lab?"

"No thanks. I dropped my last roll of film off at the drugstore last night after I took Carey home." She frowned. "I'm worried about her, Steve. That close call on the old stairs yesterday is still bothering her."

"I know. I saw it in her eyes today. But she'll get over it, Marty. She has too much going for her to let something like that get her down for very long."

He picked up a photo and examined it closely. "I wish Carey would have come with us. I need all the feedback I can get."

They pored over the photos, almost forgetting to sip their icy Cokes. Their comments ranged from, "No—no—not that one, please!" to "The angle's good but the focus isn't sharp enough."

Eventually Steve settled on Marty's favorite: the distant highway faintly blurred, visibly contrasting with the sharp cliff edges and tall tower cutting into the sky.

"You have an unusual eye for mood and feeling," he said, startling her. "It's much better than my own."

"Oh, no," she protested. "It's your way of seeing things that makes me notice details I've never seen before."

Steve gathered the photos from the table. "Maybe we're good for each other." He opened his portfolio. "Partners in a fuller sense of the word than we realized."

He looked at her expectantly and Marty blushed, covering her confusion by reaching for her Coke with lowered eyes. She stirred the drink with her straw. "Maybe so. I'm not sure."

They finished their Cokes and went out to Steve's Datsun. Noticing the lights from the drugstore across the Plaza, Marty hesitated. She gestured toward the store. "Could we walk over to see if my film's ready?"

Steve set his portfolio on the seat. "Of course," he agreed quickly. He came around to her side and reached for her hand. "I'd like to see them too."

They crossed the wide parking lot and went inside the brightly lit store. The clerk at the counter was apologetic. "I'm sorry," he said. "Our film orders won't be in until morning."

Disappointment, coupled with a feeling of relief, rushed through Marty. *Steve's photos are so perfect . . . so right. While mine. . .*

They were quiet as they returned to the car, each deep in thought. "Marty," Steve said suddenly, "I keep thinking about those lights we saw that night."

"What about them?"

"I don't know. They just don't seem to fit with the photos." He opened the car door and took out the portfolio he'd set on the seat. "I keep feeling I'm missing something— something important."

Marty felt uneasy also. "Shall we look at them again?"

Steve nodded. "Are you game?"

"Sure. If there's something we're missing—"

She giggled as they stepped through Guido's wide front door. "They'll wonder what we forgot."

"It doesn't matter," Steve said. They returned to the table by the window and once again spread the photos across its shining surface.

Marty leaned forward eagerly. What was it they had missed? Something important? Something vital?

"The lights," she said suddenly. "They seem to have come from inside the house. But these windows are boarded."

A long, low whistle came from Steve's lips. "I think you have something there, Marty. But wait. The lights could have come from outside the house. Someone could have been on the veranda."

"But there were two. As I recall, one was higher than the other Steve, look at this." Marty's fingers rested on the tower window. "The boards over this one have been torn away."

She probed for details. "One of the lights we saw must have come from this window."

Her brown eyes met his blue ones. "Steve, this house isn't just an empty shell waiting for destruction. There's something inside. I'm sure of it."

Chapter 13 / Selling Ad Space—Again

Marty wakened early. A dullness lay over the day. Her warm breath fogged the window, obscuring her usual morning view. Her gaze moved to the picture of the house on the rock. Steve had said that man's life foundation went deep because he had built it upon the truth of God's Word.

With sudden resolution, Marty pushed back the blankets. She'd begin her day with a Psalm. She jumped up and unzipped the backpack where she'd left her Bible. Before she slipped back inside her blanket nest, she turned the thermostat to a higher temperature. Welcome warmth poured into the room as she began reading, "Psalm 18—A Psalm of Enduring Love."

The first few verses made little sense to her. But the verse, "In my anguish I cried to the Lord, and he answered by setting me free," spoke to her almost audibly.

"That's like me, God," she whispered. "You came to me when I needed you. You set me free from my sins."

She continued reading. "The Lord is with me; I will not be afraid. What can man do to me?"

Traci—she was afraid of Traci. The animosity in her eyes revealed what was in her heart. But Marty's God was saying He was with her, that He was her Helper. That she could look in triumph on her enemies.

That means I don't have to be afraid to sell ad space today, she thought. *My God is my helper. He'll walk beside me.*

"Oh, God, you are so wonderful!" She closed her eyes. "Thank you, Lord, that you are my Refuge—my strong Rock. I love you."

She opened her eyes. The moisture was disappearing from her window, and a weak ray of morning sun added its own special brand of encouragement.

Marty leapt out of bed and donned her black denims, turquoise sweater, and matching earrings. She looked in the mirror as she brushed her hair, bringing out its golden color, noting how her amber eyes reflected light from the morning.

I'm almost pretty, she thought somewhat surprised. *I wonder if Steve will think so too. . .*

A glow ran through her. Last night he'd asked her to meet him in the journalism building before classes began. He wanted her to help him with the bulletin board, arranging the photos of the cliff house in the most attractive way.

Marty's father dropped her off at the school a half hour later. She looked eagerly and spotted Steve's car in the parking lot, then hurried inside.

The building held a different atmosphere now than it would later; only an occasional student scurried down the hall, intent on some early morning task. There was no loitering, no flicker of interested glances as boy met girl.

The journalism room was strangely quiet also—no humming computers, no clacking typewriter keys, no voices of harried staff members and teacher.

Marty found Steve in front of the bulletin-board display, his photos spread on a nearby table. He looked up as she came in, welcome sparkling from his blue eyes.

"I'm glad you made it," he said warmly.

Together they arranged and rearranged, criticized and

complimented one another's ideas. The room filled with interested students gathering close to offer suggestions or admiration. Mr. Hollister joined them before the first bell rang.

"I like what you've done, Steve. You, too, Marty." His big hand clasped Marty's shoulder. "I'm excusing you from class today," he told her. "I need those ad spaces filled right away."

A cold dread clasped icy fingers around Marty's stomach. She looked up and caught Steve's concerned gaze. No words were exchanged, but Marty suddenly felt comforted. Steve's God—her God now—would be her Helper—her Refuge. *And I won't have to work with Traci,* she thought with relief. *I'll be away from the cold glare of her eyes.*

The sun had broken through the morning overcast by the time Marty finished her telephone calls to several of the area merchants. Her first stop was Creative Creations. She hesitated in the doorway and nervously shifted the portfolio under her arm. A basket arrangement of colorful chrysanthemums and twining ivy in the window caught her eye, distracting her.

She remembered the Flower Mill ad she'd seen in the sample yearbook Mr. Hollister had had them look over the day before. She could picture ivy artfully decorating the basket handle and then spilling around the shop name. She knew exactly how the completed ad could look in the yearbook and felt her confidence rise.

"You like my arrangement?" a pleasant voice behind her asked.

Marty turned. A woman with a cheery open face smiled at her. Beside her stood a man with a salt-and-pepper beard, brown suspenders and faded blue denims.

Marty's expectant confidence evaporated. "Mr. Merwyn!" she gasped. "I didn't expect to see you here. How are you?"

"Fine, thank you." Mr. Merwyn's steady gray eyes probed hers. Would she meet with his approval today?

She lifted her chin bravely and addressed the woman. "I'm Marty Bauer from the Sherwood High School yearbook. I talked with you about buying ad space a little while ago."

"Wait," Mr. Merwyn said. "I'd like your opinion." He pointed to the chrysanthemum arrangement in the window. "I'm wanting something special for my daughter, and you've expressed interest in her. Do you think she'd like that?"

"Tell me about her," Marty said softly. "What does she look like? What does she care most about?"

Mr. Merwyn hooked his thumbs beneath his brown suspenders. "She's little, not too tall. Her hair is darker than yours but not too dark."

"Her smile? Is it like yours?"

"She has a dimple." One hand came out and touched his bearded cheek. "Right here. When she smiles it comes out like sunshine after rain." He shook his head. "She doesn't smile like she used to."

"What does she enjoy? sewing? art?"

"Mostly it's her two little girls. Always has been. Before she got sick she was always doing special things for them—making gingerbread men, playing with them, running through the sprinkler. Now she mostly reads them stories, plays the piano—" One hand brushed across his eyes and Marty's throat tightened.

"I—I don't think the yellow chrysanthemums would be quite right. She needs something gentler." She looked at the woman. "Do you have pink roses? Little sprigs of baby's breath?"

The woman nodded. "I'm Mrs. Thatcher. But you may call me Ruth if you'd like. Come into the back room," she invited. "We'll put together something she'll enjoy."

They stepped through polished swinging gates into the next room. Flowers of varied hues and green ferns filled large containers. There was a deep sink in the corner and a large table with scraps of ribbon and bits of baby breath.

The good smell of the outdoors filled the tiny room. Marty sniffed curiously, picked up the subdued scent of roses, the pungent scent of fern.

"I do my arranging here." Ruth gestured toward the table. "Go ahead, Marty. It is Marty, isn't it?"

"Yes." Marty hesitated, not knowing what was expected of her. Was this woman suggesting she make the arrangement for Mr. Merwyn's daughter?

"Go ahead," the woman repeated. "I'd like to see what you can do. There's foam soaking in the sink and vases in the cupboard beside it." She smiled. "You seem to have a feel for what Mr. Merwyn is looking for. I'll look over what you do—make suggestions if you need them."

She stepped out of the room and Marty was left alone. She went over to the sink and opened the cabinet. There were a variety of vases to choose from, some large and ornate.

Marty chose a small white vase and set it on the table. As she selected bits of baby's breath and several pink rosebuds, she smiled ironically. *What a strange way to be selling yearbook advertisements*, she mused.

Pressing the stems of the buds into place, she added tiny sprays of baby's breath. But as she observed the arrangement, she felt disappointment. *It needs something,* she puzzled. *I know. Something green, something besides fern.*

A sprig of miniature ivy caught her attention. She reached for it and a pink rose that was taller than the buds she'd already chosen. She put the rose in place and wove the ivy strand around the slender stem, then stepped back to look at it.

She liked the way the ivy drew the tall rose and the small

buds clustered at the base together. The arrangement reminded her in a gentler way of the subtle glow of a single candle burning in a darkened room, its reflection multiplied and glinting against polished wood.

"I approve," Ruth said from the doorway.

Marty picked up the vase and handed it to her. "Do you think Mr. Merwyn will like it?"

"Let's ask him."

Marty opened the gate and joined Ruth and Mr. Merwyn. Ruth set the arrangement on the counter as Marty held her breath, watching Mr. Merwyn's face. A longing rose inside her. She hoped he would approve of her work.

His nod was slow in coming. He reached out his hand and touched the center rose, his big forefinger looking out of place against the soft petals.

"It's like my girl," he said at last. He pulled his wallet out of his pocket. "How much do I owe you?"

He counted out the bills, then turned to Marty. "I'm wanting to buy ad space in your high school yearbook, Marty. Come by my store later today and I'll give you a check."

He looked at Ruth. "I suggest you do the same. Somehow I feel those ads are well worth the asking price." He picked up the flowers and strode out of the store.

Marty stared after him.

"He's a hurting man," Ruth said softly, "and you touched his heart. I'm glad you were here. My arrangement would have been all wrong.

"Now about buying ad space." She reached for her checkbook. "I'm making an additional contribution," she said. "I sense you don't want payment for doing Mr. Merwyn's arrangement, so I'll even us up this way."

"But I didn't even show you the ad selections," Marty protested. She opened the portfolio she'd laid on the counter.

"And I have an idea that would enhance your ad. If I could—"

Ruth shook her head. "You don't need to explain. With your flare for detail and balance, you won't need me telling you what to do. I trust you to put together an ad that will be just right."

She laid the check on the counter. "Thank you, Marty. If you ever want to do part-time work in my flower shop, call me."

Outside on the street with the late autumn sunshine surrounding her, Marty had to restrain herself from doing a Tarzan yell. Instead, she hugged her portfolio close to her heart.

As she hurried down the street, she couldn't help but contrast this day with the day she'd run away from Mr. Merwyn's store. That day she'd utterly failed, fighting twin dragons named "Anger" and "Hopelessness." Today she'd sold two ads and gotten additional funds for the yearbook besides.

"I can't believe it's really happened," she whispered to the fallen leaves skittering across the pavement. The words of the Psalm she'd read that morning flashed through her mind. Something about God being her Helper, her Refuge, her Rock.

She went several paces past the drugstore before she remembered the film she needed to pick up. Retracing her steps, she pushed the front door open.

The drugstore was almost empty of customers, the clerk behind the counter drowsy and uncommunicative. He went into the pharmacy section and returned, handing her the envelope. Marty removed the photos and arranged them on the counter. Faint disappointment stirred in her as she viewed the ones she'd taken of the old house. Steve's were much better.

Surprisingly, the one she'd snapped of Carey on the stairs

to nowhere appealed to her more than the others. Carey's teasing smile had a happy carefree look that went with the floating stairway. Her brown hair contrasted with her blue eyes, which matched the sky behind her.

Not yet the sliding earth and the wrenching of wood. Not yet Carey's wild cry or her own panic rising inside her.

The clerk returned and Marty put the photos back inside the envelope and paid for them. Then she took out the negatives and held them to the light. She handed the clerk the one of Carey, "I'd like an enlargement made of this, please."

She felt a sense of satisfaction as she walked back to school. The afternoon was warmer now and she slipped off her jacket, throwing it across her arm. She glanced at her watch, noting the time. If she hurried she'd be in time for "πr^2."

Her pace quickened. Her breath came in gasps as she hurried up the slight incline in front of the school sign. She slowed before she reached the top, digging into her purse for a comb to smooth her fly-away hair.

Her hand froze in midair.

Traci stood with her back to Marty; the carefully trimmed camellia tree that grew on the edge of the school grounds was between her and the school building.

An older man leaned against the tree, looking intently into Traci's face. Marty sensed at once something vaguely familiar in the set of his shoulders, the angle of his dark head. Had she seen him before?

Traci shook her head violently and looked down at the ground. The man leaned forward and Marty stiffened.

The man's hand came out and forced Traci's face upward. At the same moment he looked up and Marty gazed full into his lean, hard face.

Fear rose inside her. She recognized those metallic eyes.

Were they Traci's own? Or were they some specter from her own past come to haunt her?

Marty didn't wait to find out. She turned and ran back down the street.

Chapter 14 / Destruction

Marty paused outside her house and looked at the empty garage, the blank windows.

Her hand slid inside her purse. She fingered her house key, then let it slip through her fingers. Instead of unlocking the door and going inside, she sat down on the front steps.

The neighborhood was silent; none of the schools had as yet discharged their hoardes of children. A car passed on the street and the community slept on, dozing in the early afternoon.

Marty's chin jerked as she heard a faint yip from the house next door. *Thunder*. . .

She jumped to her feet and crossed the yard. Thunder ran along the back of the velvet loveseat in front of the window in his house. He saw her looking in and whined entreatingly. He reared onto his hind legs, beating a rapid staccato with his paws against the windowpane.

Marty stepped forward. "I'm sorry, Thunder. We're both alone—and lonely. I can't get in—and you can't get out." She sat down on the grass and crossed her ankles, Indian style. She leaned forward. "But if it helps, we can talk."

The white poodle seemed to understand. He stopped his

rapid pawing and stared through the glass, his dark eyes gleaming with excitement.

"Where are your ribbons, Thunder? Did you run off again, play in the dirt?" Marty sighed. "I haven't had a wonderful day, either."

She tipped her head back, lifted thick amber hair off her neck. "Oh, Thunder, today started out so wonderfully well. And then . . . then . . ."

She leaned forward, pushed her own nose close to the glass. Thunder's small pink tongue aimed at her nose close to the glass.

"Don't, Thunder," Marty remonstrated. "You're smudging Mrs. Rusk's clean windows."

Thunder paid no attention. He continued his inelegant licking, his eyes full of love and appeal.

"Traci and that—that man," Marty continued. "He reminded me of someone, Thunder, but I don't know who! He looked menacing. And he saw me—almost seemed to recognize me, or something about me. That's why I came home instead of going back to school."

She rested her elbows on her crossed legs, put her chin on her folded hands. "I shouldn't have run away. But I sensed danger."

Thunder's entire body began to wag back and forth, back and forth. He yipped a sharp welcoming bark and Marty turned. Lillian Rusk stood a few paces behind her, smiling at them.

"It looks like Thunder found a friend when he needed one," she said. "I'm glad."

Marty jumped to her feet. She brushed off the back of her jeans, her cheeks flushed with embarrassment.

"I thought Thunder needed to talk, but it turned out to be the other way around," she said self-consciously.

Mrs. Rusk appeared not to notice her discomfort. "I'll go inside and let him out. He's been alone all day."

Thunder leaped off the back of the loveseat and disappeared from Marty's view as Lillian went up the walk and opened the door. Thunder exploded through the open doorway and rushed at Marty. He danced around and around her, leaping and yipping his joy.

"He did too have something to say," Mrs. Rusk said, laughing. "And you're the one he wants to say it to."

"Thunder, you're a silly dog, but I love you."

Marty sat down on the lawn and Thunder jumped into her lap, his tiny feet scratching against her arm. His head tipped backward, brushing his damp nose against her cheek and chin.

"He knows you're his friend," Mrs. Rusk approved. She opened her purse. "Marty, I have an extra house key I'd like you to have. That way if you're here when we aren't"—she laughed softly—"and Thunder needs to talk, you can open the door and let him out."

Marty stared at the key Mrs. Rusk dropped into her palm. "Oh, Mrs. Rusk, are you sure you want to do that?"

"Of course, I'm sure. I know you and your family. Know you're to be trusted. Besides it's good for neighbors to have one another's key, don't you think? One never knows what might happen."

She disappeared into her house. Marty looked down at the white poodle, vibrating with happiness on her lap. Thunder lifted his nose, thrusting his pink tongue against her cheek.

"I'm not really sure whether talking is the name of your game, Thunder," she said ruefully. "Seems like kissing is more your speed."

Marty and Thunder spent the afternoon on the lawn together. In spite of a touch of autumn chill, Marty took her books out of her pack and tried concentrating on homework while Thunder roamed around the yard, sniffing among the marigolds in the Rusks' flower beds.

A tortoise-shell colored cat ventured near, whipping its tail in invitation. Thunder accepted with alacrity, chasing the feline up the slender trunk of a leaning maple. The cat stared down in regal disdain at Thunder scrabbling against the bark. He leaped and barked in frustration until Marty made him be quiet. She picked him up in her arms, soothing him, while the cat backed down the trunk, then ran and leaped the board fence at the back of the yard.

"Don't fret, Thunder," Marty whispered to the agitated poodle. "She just doesn't play your game by the same rules you do."

Thunder went back to snuffling in the marigold bed, Marty to perusing her opened books. Gradually the fears that had aroused when she'd seen the stranger talking with Traci dissipated. A sense of peace enveloped her as the history of Peter the Great in Russia came alive from the pages of her book, restoring her perspective.

That evening, she talked with Steve on the telephone. He was as excited and pleased as she about her meeting with Mrs. Thatcher and Mr. Merwyn. "But you should have come back to school, Marty, and told Mr. Hollister yourself. I'm sure the man you saw with Traci behind the camellia didn't mean you any harm."

Marty wasn't convinced. "Maybe he didn't," she said. "But I'm not sure. Anyway, I had a relaxing afternoon in the yard. Thunder and I talked."

Steve and Marty's conversation wandered into trivia. They chatted a while longer, exchanging bits and pieces about their taste in music, food, and the oddities surrounding their respective families.

"I'm the only one here that likes photography," Steve confided. "Sometimes that makes me feel like an oddball, makes me glad I met you."

"Did the other classes like your display?" Marty asked.

"Yes. I made a few changes, though. Would you like to

meet me early again tomorrow? I'd like your opinion about what I did.''

They agreed to a before-class meeting and hung up. That night Marty wakened to raindrops pelting against her window and water gushing through the gutters.

After breakfast the next morning, she donned vinyl raingear and headed for her father's car.

He was waiting behind the wheel, smiling at her through the glass. He backed out of the driveway slowly, the heavy sluicing rain on the windshield cutting visibility.

He dropped her as close to the entrance to the high school as possible, and Marty ran for the door. She popped through the entryway and stood silently, watching the water dripping off her coat, making little puddles at her feet.

A couple of girls were beside their lockers, shaking rain out of their hair. They headed for the restroom while Marty shoved her raingear into her locker and hurried to the journalism room to meet Steve.

He came toward her in the hall, his hair dark with dampness, sleek and neatly combed. He held out his arm and Marty took it.

They consciously adapted their footsteps to march together as they entered the J room arm-in-arm, "Hut—two—three—four. Hut—two—three—four—" Steve chanted.

They halted abruptly, shock silencing their tongues. The bulletin board displaying Steve's photos was marred beyond recognition. The various photos of the house on the cliff hung in tatters, slashed into shreds by some sharp object.

Steve dropped Marty's arm and ran to it. He stood in front of the bulletin board, numbly fingering the ugly slashed edges of his prized photographs.

A huge hammer seemed to slam into Marty's stomach. Marty's insides began to churn. She felt sick. It was unbelievable. As she stood there, her gaze probed for clues as to who could have done this horrible thing.

Nothing else in the room had been touched. Only the board and overflowing wastebasket held mute evidence of a hand bent on apparent mindless destruction.

Marty went to Steve, touched his arm. "Oh, Steve," she whispered, "I'm so sorry. Who could have done such a thing?"

Steve's stunned eyes met Marty's. "I don't know," he said slowly. "But I'm going to find out." He gestured toward the wastebasket and board. "This—this destruction is senseless. What would be the motive?"

"It isn't a total loss," Marty ventured. "You have the negatives. You can develop them."

"Do I?"

A horrible thought came to Marty's mind. Steve must have been on the same wavelength; they rushed together into the darkroom. The chemicals still sat on the counters, the enlargers along the wall were untouched.

But the file folders containing Steve's negatives were gone. They searched every wastebasket and every drawer where someone might have shoved them in a hurry. No corner went unsearched. But the negatives of the old cliff house were nowhere to be found.

The first bell rang and the J room filled with shocked students and an unbelieving Mr. Hollister. It was hard for Marty to slip away to her Civics class. Unanswered questions plagued her. They had nothing to do with the ancient Peter the Great or how the House of Congress functioned. They dealt instead with a stunned look in a young man's blue eyes, an ancient house overlooking a gravel pit and lights that blinked on and off in the night.

Marty laid her head down on her desk, shutting out the drone of the teacher's voice. Crazy mixed-up images marched through her head like bits and pieces of a jigsaw puzzle strewn out on a table. Some turned upside down were without color and distinctive only because of their shapes:

a missing antique dollhouse, a cut-glass bowl, a miniature rocking chair found beneath an upside-down tree, an ancient brooding house suspended over a cliff.

Somehow she felt she had all the pieces but couldn't fit them together. Or was there a missing piece hidden in a forgotten corner?

Something niggled at her: the man with the metallic eyes menacing Traci behind the camellia tree. Was that the hidden piece? Her fears in the night, the storm—had it become changed and unrecognizable with the passing years? Did it somehow belong with the puzzle pieces strewn on the table?

Mrs. Arnold's hand was cool on her forehead. "Marty," she said, "are you all right?"

Marty sat up and blinked. She looked around in confusion. The room was empty. She flushed in embarrassment. "Did I—was I asleep?"

"I think you must have been. You were so still." Mrs. Arnold's eyes probed Marty's face. "Are you sure you're not ill?"

"No. I mean yes. I'm not sick." She gathered her books into a neat pile and stood. "Thank you for your concern, Mrs. Arnold."

She hurried out into the hall.

The yearbook classroom looked just as it had when Marty had left it before the day's first bell had rung. She slipped into her usual seat, deliberately avoiding looking at Traci next to her. A sober Mr. Hollister stood beside the ruined bulletin board display.

The usually high-spirited yearbookers were subdued. Questioning looks and whispers were everywhere as Mr. Hollister's gray gaze roamed the room. For a moment his eye caught Marty's; an encouraging smile touched his lips.

The last bell rang and the class stilled.

"Some of you already know—others don't—but an act

of vandalism was performed right here in this room, either last night or early this morning." Mr. Hollister pointed to the slashed bits of photos still clinging to the board.

"And that wasn't all," he continued. "This bulletin board held photos that had an excellent chance of placing in the contest. They're gone. Whoever slashed them into strips also took the negatives."

A gasp swept through the room. Everyone started talking at once.

"Wait." Mr. Hollister held up his hand.

The room quieted.

"I chose to leave this ruined display just as it is because"—once again his eyes searched Marty's classmates—"I believe this was done by one of our own students. I want this ugliness to remain before their eyes today. That's all. Continue with your assignments." He sat down.

Marty stared at the board. The ripped photos blurred before her gaze. *Oh, Steve, I'm sorry. So very, very sorry.*

"As if any of us would do a thing like that," Traci muttered in a low, irritated voice. "Who does he think he is, anyway?"

Marty looked up from the layout spread in front of her. "He's our teacher," she said quietly. The pupils of the hard, cold eyes staring into her own seemed to sharpen, then contract. *Like glittering birds of prey,* Marty thought.

Out loud she said, "Whoever sneaked in here and shredded those photos needs to see how it looks to the rest of us, needs to understand how it makes others feel."

Traci's long lashes lowered over her eyes. Her shoulders jerked as she turned her back to Marty.

For a moment Marty sat very still. Then she leaned toward Traci, whispering, "I saw you off grounds yesterday. What's the matter? What is it you're trying to hide?"

Traci neither turned nor acknowledged Marty's whispered words. She poked her face into a book and refused to show by another word or action that Marty even existed.

The hour was one of the most difficult Marty had ever experienced. Her subdued classmates and Traci's cold, defensive presence at her elbow, combined with the shreds of Steve's dreams and hard work facing her whenever she looked toward the front, were troubling, frustrating.

Mr. Hollister stopped at her side before the dismissal bell rang. Marty opened her portfolio and gave him the checks she'd collected from Mr. Merwyn and Creative Creation.

His hand on her shoulder was approving. "Mrs. Thatcher called me this morning," he said in a low voice. "She complimented me on the way we did our business— and you. She said you were an asset. I'm proud of you, Marty."

Marty appreciated his compliment but almost wished he hadn't said it right then. The stiff shoulders of her nearby antagonist reminded her she had an enemy. Marty knew Traci had heard every word Mr. Hollister had said.

The bell rang and Traci left without a backward glance, brushing past Steve in the open doorway. He looked intently into her face, raised a questioning eyebrow, then looked around the room. Marty waved and he came over to her.

Marty felt his tension. She saw it in the thrust of his jaw, in a muscle that twitched in his cheek.

"I've been running this whole scenario over and over in my mind this morning," he said without preamble. "Marty, you took photos of that house, too, and I'm afraid."

"Afraid?" Marty echoed. "Why?"

"I thought at first someone who didn't want contest competition destroyed the photos and took the negatives. Mr. Hollister thinks that, too. But later I got to thinking. Remember that board over the window—the one hanging loose?"

"Yes. Yes, I do. But Steve, I have several photos and

negatives of the house in my purse. They didn't destroy those!"

"They probably don't know you have them," Steve said soberly. "Would you let me keep them for you? They've destroyed mine so they won't bother me. But if they put two and two together and discover you have photos, too—Marty, you could be in danger."

"Danger! Steve, what do you mean?"

"It might be that someone doesn't want us to have evidence—evidence that we haven't as yet picked up on."

The sober look in his eyes convinced her. She looked around the room, then opened her purse. "Be careful, Steve," she warned as she pressed the envelope into his hands.

Chapter 15 / A New Entry

"Lord, I would delight in you and in your word," Marty wrote. "I would think on it day and night. But, Lord, right now I need forgiveness. My thoughts have been full of me—people—situations I can't do anything about. No wonder I'm so tense and anxious!"

Marty put her pen on her bedside stand and looked up at the new photos decorating one wall of her room. The Oregon grape with its purple berries and the scarlet vine maple branch against the blue sky added an unusual touch. The house on the rock, standing firm against the storm, still occupied the focal point. Later she would put next to it the photo she'd taken of the house poised over the gravel pit.

She smiled, then returned to her Bible and notebook. This writing Psalms into personal prayers was beginning to be an important part of her new life with Christ. She'd begun putting them into a special notebook at Mr. Wilson's suggestion. Already this week, she'd written several.

"Lord," she continued writing, "trees beside streams speak of peace, and I've been anything but peaceful these past few days—weeks really. I'm like a volcano inside ready to explode."

I am too, she thought. *Every day there's Traci and her malicious looks and Steve's disappointment. He never did get a retake of that old house to enter in the contest. And now the contest deadline is behind us.*

She uncurled her legs and wandered to the window. Rain poured against the glass. Four weeks of rain had ruined everything for Steve. Winds had torn across the countryside. Even the last gold leaves of the birch tree in Mrs. Rusk's yard and the tenacious oak leaves had been driven earthward.

Unable to return to the cliff house, he'd found another photo to enter. "But it's not what I wanted," he explained to Marty. Nor had Marty's photo of Carey on the stairs to nowhere satisfied her. She still longed for the picture she carried in her imagination—Sunny looking inside the dollhouse . . .

There were other frustrations as well. They hadn't made any headway at all in finding the dollhouse. Nor had they discovered who'd destroyed Steve's prize photos. The man behind the shrubbery remained a mystery and Traci still hated Marty.

The rain had even managed to put a damper on the football season. The one game she'd attended with Steve had turned into a mud contest, with the players sliding over each other in the field.

He hadn't asked her again.

Marty went back to her bed. Even though there'd been problems, her new relationship with God was satisfying and real. She looked at Psalm One, continued to read, then wrote:

"Lord, I choose your way. Right now I need to still myself beside the stream. Only then will I yield fruit in your season. Only then will my leaves be green, beautiful, not withered and falling to the ground.

"You're promising to watch over me, over my ways. I open my ways wide before you."

Marty sighed. Was she really opening her ways before

her God? Deep inside dark feelings and unrest still plagued her. She knew her relationship with her mother wasn't all it could be. And that wasn't all. The past month had seen a change in her friendship with Carey. For the first time in the two years they'd been together, there'd been a separation of their ways.

It was partly because Carey was spending more and more of her weekends away with her parents. But there was something else and Marty couldn't put her finger on it.

"I guess there're things I don't want to face up to, Lord," she said out loud.

The phone at her bedside rang and she picked it up.

Steve's words were brief and to the point. "Want to go to the football game with me tonight? The weatherman reports clear skys this afternoon."

"But it will be too late," Marty protested. "The field will still be a mud hole."

"True. But at least we won't have to fight the deluge coming and going. What about it? Besides, my sports editor is sick and I need some good close-ups for the sports page."

"Okay. Let's."

He hung up and for some reason Marty felt relieved and immensely cheered. She put the phone down and turned to the business of preparing her face and hair to meet the day.

Selecting a brown sweater with rosy tones she tried to decide what she'd wear to the game that night. Time ran out before she could make up her mind. She ran downstairs.

Her mother was spreading butter on her toast, a cup of coffee in front on her on the counter. She looked up as Marty came into the kitchen.

Marty couldn't help comparing her mother's vivid, well-dressed appearance with her own—her cheery red blouse matched her fingernails and contrasted with her black hair, skirt and pumps. Her own attire was pale in comparison, casual jeans and brown sweater, honey blond hair floating loose around her face.

"You're late," Marty blurted.

"I won't be going to the office until noon," her mother said. "I'm meeting someone this morning."

"Who?"

"No one you know. Someone I knew long ago."

A flicker of the apprehension Marty had felt in the early hours of the morning fluttered inside her. "Does Dad know this person?"

"No—not really."

"Is it a man?"

Her mother put her knife down. "What is this, Marty," she demanded. "The third degree?"

Marty felt her cheeks redden. "I'm sorry," she muttered. She poured herself a tall glass of orange juice and put two slices of bread into the toaster.

She sipped her juice as she waited for her toast to pop. Her mother came over to her and, in an unusual show of affection, put her arm around her shoulders. Marty stiffened.

"I shouldn't be so defensive," her mother said unexpectedly. "The person I'm meeting is someone your father never approved of. I feel weird talking about—the person."

Is it a man? Marty wanted to ask again. Fear kept her lips sealed. She took a deep breath and wished her mother would leave.

Her mother moved away. She took a sip of coffee, averting her eyes.

For the first time since she could remember, Marty felt sorry for her mother. But she didn't know how to say the words. Instead, she removed her hot toast and reached for butter and strawberry jam.

Silence. Neither one knew what to say. *Trivia, stick to trivia*, an inner voice whispered to Marty.

"Dad gone already?"

Her mother nodded. "Yes. He left before I got up. Today's job is clear over on the other side of town—Northwest Portland." She put her half-eaten slice of toast and unfinished coffee beside the sink. "I have to run."

Was that an appeal for understanding in her dark eyes as she hesitated in the open doorway? "Have a good day, Marty."

"Bye, Mom." Marty put her glass beside her mother's cup and reached for the dishcloth.

The kitchen door closed softly.

That morning the wind blew away the clouds. Marty sat in her classes, sneaking a look outside whenever she could. By afternoon the sky cleared and November sun coaxed dampness from the sodden earth, turning it into foggy steam beside the asphalt roads.

In the evening Marty paused as she dressed for her date with Steve. "I miss the stars," she whispered.

She stepped to the window, holding her nubby pink sweater vest in front of her and peered into the night sky. The deep oblong of rain-washed sky above the Rusk's house was pricked with brilliant stars. A new moon hung low on the horizon.

Turning from the window, she slipped her vest over her long-sleeved rose flowered blouse. Then she brushed her hair vigorously, bringing out the gold highlights. She laid down the brush, picked up her jacket and hurried down the stairs.

Steve was waiting for her in the living room, talking with her father. He looked up and smiled and something very close to pride washed through Marty. Steve was so tall, his thick wavy hair and bright curious eyes made him stand out wherever he happened to be. And right now "wherever" was her own home.

She knew her father approved of him, too, because he jostled her arm in a proprietory way as she stood beside him. "Take good care of my girl," he admonished Steve good-naturedly as Steve reached out his hand.

"I will, sir."

They shook hands soberly, man-to-man, and then Steve and Marty went out into the night.

"I like your dad," Steve said as they got into the car. "Where was your mom?"

Marty shrugged. "She had to work late. She called." She turned to the window. She didn't want to think about her mother, didn't want to think about the conversation they'd had that morning at breakfast.

Steve sensed her withdrawal, and turned the talk instead to school activities and Marty's new involvement with the youth group at his church.

They pulled into the student parking lot at the high school, got out and locked the doors. Steve caught Marty's hand.

"Wait," he said.

Marty's heart skipped inside her. The hand he was holding trembled.

But Steve's eyes weren't on her. His head was tipped back, his attention held by the new moon riding the horizon, the pale fragile stars competing with the parking lights.

Marty pulled on his hand. "The game's started," she reminded him. "You might miss the best shot unless we hurry."

Steve laughed. "Let's go."

They sprinted across the parking lot, and became one with the other spectators surging into the grandstand. They found places as close to the front as possible; then Steve left her, the camera dangling from his neck strap.

Both teams were already lined up on the field, ready for action. The whistle blew. Marty watched Steve stop for a word with the coach.

"Marty! Marty!"

Marty turned. Carey bounded down the grandstand

steps. Her cheeks were flushed, almost matching her red jacket. Her long brown hair bounced on her shoulders.

"Can I?" she gasped, gesturing to the space Steve had so recently vacated.

Marty nodded. A faint unease nudged her. She shifted her position, crossing her knees.

Carey flopped down onto the bench beside her. Her attention was obviously not on the football game. "Are you with Steve?" she asked.

Marty looked at her friend curiously and nodded. "What's up?"

Carey leaned forward. She looked down, her long, slender fingers fumbling with the brown purse on her lap. She lifted her head and tossed her long hair away from her collar with an impatient gesture.

"Did either you or Steve get a letter today?"

"No. Why should we?"

"Because . . . because . . . ." Carey's blue eyes wouldn't quite meet Marty's own.

"Carey," Marty entreated. "Look at me. What's wrong?"

"Nothing's wrong," Carey flared. "It's just that . . . that . . . Oh, Marty, everything's wrong! I stole your idea. But I didn't plan to steal it. It just happened."

"Carey, you're not making sense. Maybe you should take a deep breath—"

"And count to ten. Right?"

"Yes. Then start at the beginning."

Carey's words were drowned out as the crowd rose as a whole, screaming their excitement. Marty craned her neck to see what was happening on the field. She started to jump to her feet, but Carey gripped her hand, holding her back.

"The letter is from the photo contest!" she shouted into Marty's ear. "They congratulated me—said I showed unusual promise."

"What are you saying?" Marty demanded. She whirled to face her friend.

"I'm one of the top ten, Marty!" Carey cried. "They say I have a good chance to place—with honor."

There was a disappointed "ooh," and the spectators surrounding them resumed their seats. For a brief moment Carey covered her face with her hands.

She lowered her hands. "Although I didn't know it then, it began the day you mentioned you'd like to find out what happened to Mr. Merwyn's antique dollhouse for two reasons—first for his sake, then for your own."

"I remember," Marty said flatly. "Keep talking."

"You said you could picture my little sister, Sunny, peering inside it, a look of wonder on her face. 'I'd take her picture,' you said. 'I'd do a close-up and it would be yesterday meeting today. It would be a perfect entry for the contest.' "

"And you—you?"

Carey stared straight ahead. "Right after that I went to spend a weekend with my parents in Astoria. Sunny and I went exploring. We saw an antique dollhouse in this tiny shop."

Marty gasped. "Could it be Mr. Merwyn's? Do you suppose?"

"Wait. Sunny ran back to the motel room and got Dad's camera. It was so perfect, Marty. Just like you'd said it would be. And Sunny posed so beautifully."

"And then?"

"I sent it into the magazine." Her blue eyes met Marty's, begging for understanding. "But I never dreamed—"

Hurt washed over Marty. She put her own face in her hands.

Carey's hands suddenly covered hers. Marty felt Carey's hair brush her cheeks. "I've felt terrible ever since, Marty. So absolutely awful. If you can—forgive me."

Then Carey was gone.

Marty lifted her head. Only the flash of departing red gave any indication Carey had even been there.

After that it was hard for Marty to concentrate on the game. Even Steve darting around the edges of the field failed to capture her full attention.

Oh, Carey, how could you? The hurt caused by Carey's confession didn't go away and bitterness closed in around her heart.

The loudspeaker proclaimed the last remaining minute to the game, and Marty left her seat. She spotted Steve beside the coach and threaded her way through the crowd.

Steve knelt for a last camera shot and the whistle blew. He stood up and signaled her with a wave.

He joined her at the field's edge. His jeans and jacket were speckled with mud, but Marty could tell he didn't mind. His eyes flashed with excitement and accomplishment. He reached out his arm, pulling her close.

Then he lifted her chin with his forefinger. "What is it?" he asked, his eyes searching her face. "Did you see Traci?"

"No. Oh, Steve, it's worse than that! Much worse."

"Tell me."

"Not here." She clung to his arm. "In the car. We can talk then."

They held their words as they slipped and sloshed with the crowd around the edge of the muddy field. They reached the parking lot and Steve quickened his pace so Marty almost had to run to keep up. She was panting when they reached the car.

"It's a good thing you parked here instead of the other side."

"I'm sorry," Steve said, realizing she was out of breath. He opened the door for her and went around to the other side. "I guess I'm impatient to hear what happened to you tonight."

She took a deep breath, then recounted how Carey had taken her idea and entered it in the contest without saying anything. "All this time I was thinking she was distant because of her narrow escape from the gravel pit. I even convinced myself that she was thinking about—you know—the brevity of life, that sort of thing. And all this time . . ."

She looked at Steve, noting how his fingers rested against his face, covering his mouth. "Oh, Steve!" she cried. "She not only stole my ideas and didn't tell me, she knew we were searching for Mr. Merwyn's dollhouse and never said a word. I don't understand."

"She tricked you by deliberately concealing information," Steve murmured softly. "And now I'm wondering. I've been blaming Traci for slashing my display to bits. Maybe it was Carey."

"No!" Marty cried. "She's not that kind of person."

She stopped. *She wasn't honest with you,* her thoughts whispered. *She stole your idea, kept the existence of the dollhouse she'd seen from you, even secretly entered the contest, though winning meant nothing to her.*

Into her mind flashed a picture: Carey with razor blade in hand, shredding Steve's photographs into ugly strips. Then Marty saw Carey as she'd seen her that night, her face in her hands, her brown hair spilling around her shoulders.

"She did ask me to forgive her," Marty whispered.

"I shouldn't have said what I did," Steve said contritely. "I really don't think it. It's just that—" He changed the subject. "I'd like to see that photo she took. I wonder if she still has the negative."

"We could ask."

Steve reached across the seat, taking her hand. "It wouldn't be wise for us to take this too hard," he said. "The contest was doomed as far as I was concerned when I lost my best entry. I've already accepted that.

"We need to go on from here. Something good may

come from Carey's weekend escapade yet. Perhaps that antique dollhouse is the one Mr. Merwyn and the police are searching for. If it is"—a glimmer of a smile brushed his lips—"then we're onto something."

Chapter 16 / Thunder Runs Away

The telephone rang and Marty burrowed deeper under her blankets, trying to keep the day from intruding into her consciousness.

"Marty!"

She turned onto her side, reaching for the slim white telephone on her nightstand. Her voice felt thick, unused to the morning. "Hello."

She recognized Steve's voice. "Marty, did I wake you up?"

"Yes. But it's all right." She squinted at the clock on her wall. "I have to start moving or I'll be late for class. What's up?"

"I talked with Carey," Steve said unexpectedly.

The sleep dissolved from Marty's brain.

"She brought over her negatives," Steve said. "I'm going to develop them this morning, find out if the dollhouse is possibly Mr. Merwyn's."

"But—"

"I've misjudged Carey," Steve said softly. "I sense a genuine remorse in her. She really does love you, Marty. She said you were her best friend."

"Best friend," Marty spluttered. She jerked her spread aside and got up. "I have to go now, Steve. I'm glad you talked to Carey. Maybe those negatives will give you the lead you need. I hope so."

"Wait," Steve insisted. "Marty, I think your attitude is wrong."

Marty bristled. "My attitude?"

"You're holding onto your hurt," he persisted. "You need to let go of it, give it to God, or it'll turn to anger."

Marty's gaze went to her picture of the house on the rock. *The foolish man had built his house on an unstable foundation.* Was that what she was doing?

Her reply was slow in coming. "Right now I'm confused, Steve. I have to go. Thanks for calling."

She replaced the phone on its stand and sat down abruptly on the edge of the bed. Her Bible lay beside the telephone and Marty picked it up.

She opened to the Psalms. "There must be something about friends," she whispered. "David must have written at least one psalm about them."

She leafed through the pages, scanning the titles, then turned to the concordance in the back of her Bible. Psalm 41:9: "Even my close friend, whom I trusted, he who shared my bread, has lifted up his heel against me."

Except Carey hadn't been malicious. Not like that. "But David's friend hurt him," she whispered. "And so did Jesus' disciples. David and Jesus both felt the pain of someone they were close to, someone they loved, letting them down."

A lump swelled into her throat. She remembered Jesus' words to His disciples in the garden, "My soul is overwhelmed with sorrow to the point of death. Stay here and keep watch with me."

Except they hadn't. They'd gone to sleep and Jesus had been left alone. The friends He was closest to let Him down in His hour of need.

"But He loved them," her heart whispered. "His Word says He loved them until the very end. Oh, God, I need a love like that—a love that won't quit, no matter what. Carey—"

Her watch beeped and she leaped to her feet. There wasn't time now for a leisurely shower and outfit selection. She pulled a sweater over her head and reached for her denims.

That afternoon she stopped by Steve's desk.

His eyes lit up when he saw her. "I was hoping you'd stop by," he said. He handed her a sheet of tiny black and white photos.

Marty looked intently at the one Steve had circled. The antique dollhouse was exactly as Marty remembered. She recognized the slope of the roof with its tiny shakes, the perfectly crafted bay windows. Sunny's profile was silhouetted against the outside of the house as she peered inside, her forefinger pushing aside the miniature curtains.

"It's the one I saw in Mr. Merwyn's store!" Marty exclaimed. "I'm sure it is."

She sat down in the chair beside Steve's desk, her stomach a cold lump. Carey had accurately captured what Marty had longed to do—Sunny's profile, her look of awe and wonder.

Her eyes met Steve's. "Have you told Mr. Merwyn?"

"Not yet. I wanted you to see them first. So, there's a good chance the lost is found." He leaned forward, gently tapping his finger against her nose. "You don't look exactly happy."

"I'm sorry."

"Me, too. I shouldn't have said what I did about your attitude this morning. I know what it's like when a friend pulls away from you—keeps you at a distance."

Marty took a deep breath. "It hurts," she confessed. "I think it's mostly that Carey and I had been so close, shared so much together. And then all of a sudden we weren't. It got me to thinking, Steve. Jesus' disciples left Him alone when He needed them most. Instead of following Him to the cross they followed at a distance."

"Yes," Steve agreed. "They did something much worse than what Carey did. Remember Judas? He was Jesus' friend, too, and look what he did. He betrayed Him to the enemy with a kiss."

"The kiss of death," Marty murmured.

She stood up, trying to shake off her heavy thoughts.

"Want to get together after school?" Steve asked.

Marty shook her head. "I don't think so. It's not that I'm upset now," she hastily assured him. "I just need some time to think. Dad car-pooled to work this morning so I have the car. If the weather holds I might go out to the old house, sit underneath that old cedar tree."

"If you do, be careful," Steve entreated. "Promise you won't go near the house? All the rain we've had couldn't have done much for that slope it's teetering on."

"I know. I saw the backhoe gnawing into the bank yesterday, too. Poor old house."

"I'd like to photograph it before it falls," Steve said thoughtfully. "But if I go over after school, I'll stay clear of your cedar tree—give you time alone in your nest."

The bell rang and he reached out, giving her hand a reassuring squeeze.

The rest of the day crawled for Marty. It bothered her that she didn't see Carey, but in a way she was glad. She needed time to sort out her feelings, time to think things through. She knew she needed to work things out with her God.

Marty stopped by the house to change her clothes after school. As she ran up the path, she noticed large puffy gray clouds pushing their rounded heads above the horizon. A light wind quivered the bare branches of the leafless birch, the broad-leafed maple.

A faint howling trembled the air and Marty smiled. *Thunder—I wonder if he's alone, needs to talk.*

She let herself into the house and hurried up the stairs. She picked up yesterday's jeans lying on the chair, hesitated a moment before selecting her navy hooded sweatshirt.

Thunder's mournful howls arrested her attention the moment she let herself out the front door. "Okay, Thunder," she muttered, "I'll stop long enough for us to say 'Hi.' "

Swinging her backpack stuffed with Bible, notebook and camera across her shoulder, she ran across the lawn to the Rusk house. The key Lillian Rusk had given her turned in the lock.

Thunder charged her like a small catapult, leaping into her arms, licking her cheeks. "Hey, calm down, little friend," Marty said, patting his fuzzy topknot, trying to rearrange his red ribbon. "It won't do for you to get all bent out of shape."

But Thunder was past being reasoned with. When Marty set him on the kitchen floor, he raced around and around the room and yipped in loud, high-spirited fashion.

"Little Buddy, I have to go."

Thunder sprinted to the door and stood in front of it, his entire body quivering in anticipation.

"Oh, I give up," Marty groaned.

She took a piece of scratch paper from the kitchen desk and scribbled a hasty note: *Thunder going nuts. Took him with me for a drive. Hope you don't mind. Marty.*

Thunder knew without being told that Marty was leaving in the red Volvo parked in the driveway. He raced to it and stood trembling until Marty opened the door. He rushed past her, leaping inside and racing back and forth on the front seat.

Marty heaved a huge sigh. "I think you're more trouble than you're worth."

The poodle quieted as she pulled out into the street. He

edged over to the window on the passenger side and looked out. Marty turned on the radio. She winced as the Grand Ole Opera played their opening chords, then adjusted the knob to a station more to her liking.

She leaned back, enjoying the music of Steve Taylor and the feel of the road beneath her. She rolled through town and onto the highway, slowing as she passed the onion flats.

The gravel pit was without activity, the house above it remote and desolate. Thunder sensed her tension and whined softly.

"We're going into the country, Thunder," Marty said. "I've brought my Bible and you're going to be quiet, aren't you?"

Thunder yowled and Marty shrugged. "I probably should have left you home to howl your head off, make the neighbors mad. I don't know why I'm such a softie."

Thunder gave a "yip" of agreement and bounced on the seat, scrabbling his paws against the armrest. They turned off on the country road and parked at the usual wide spot. Thunder dashed out without invitation as Marty opened the door. He sprinted several yards, then turned, squatted on his hind legs in an upright position, waiting for her.

Marty picked up her pack from the seat and started down the road. The white poodle dropped to all fours and danced beside her. They crossed the field, their feet sloshing in the sodden ground.

"The woods are almost ugly this time of year," Marty observed. "Even the oak leaves are gone since Steve and I were here."

Marty grimaced. The cedar hedge was the same, except rainwater stood in a little pool between the roots where she had once sat.

Thunder stuck an inquisitive nose into the water, took several laps, then rushed down the path Marty and Steve had followed the night they had seen the lights.

Marty followed the dog at a more leisurely pace, her eyes on the lofty monarch hanging precariously close to the cliff's edge. Thick heavy clouds in the west blocked the sun's rays from touching the house and drew Marty's attention.

They billowed high above the horizon, resembling great steeples carved out of ice. The sun gleaming behind them and a bank of intense gray clouds pillowed at their feet accentuated their snowy whiteness.

Marty let her mind return to childhood as she watched the shifting forms. She saw Winnie-the-Pooh leaning against a rabbit cage. The high winds changed and Winnie-the-Pooh was transformed into a rooster with a misshapen comb.

Her gaze roamed the skies. The patriarch Moses, Mickey Mouse, a white poodle with a fuzzy topknot . . .

She jumped back into the present. "Thunder," she called, "where are you?"

But the white poodle who had proudly led the way was nowhere to be seen. Marty began to run. The path turned from soft turf to slick mud and she slowed. Had Thunder come this way or had he been sidetracked by an animal scent?

She bent down and examined the mud. Thunder's tiny pawprints still pointed forward, leading to the house above the pit. Marty quickened her pace. Her tennis shoes slithered through the mud, turning browner with every step she took.

Marty topped the mound where the upside-down tree stood, a silent sentinel . . . waiting, watching.

She parted her lips to call Thunder's name but the sound was silenced before it was ever begun. Marty bit her lip, wondering why the setting seemed alien to ordinary sounds made by ordinary people.

A shaft of sunshine appeared between the clouds. Caught in the light, the house seemed more formidable than ever. Its shadow slid long across the wet grass. The sun heightened the detail of each architectural curve, revealing tiny broken panes of colored glass in the window where the board hung askew.

Something was different. Marty gasped. The boards that had covered the tower window were gone. The front door stood wide open. Even as she watched, Thunder darted through the opening and disappeared into the darkness.

This time the cry rising to her lips wasn't silenced. "Thunder!"

The little dog failed to reappear. The door he'd rushed through slammed shut. The sound reverberated across the empty space.

Marty clasped her hands over her ears. "Thunder!" she shrieked.

Once again she began to run, the sky ahead of her darkening ominously. She raced down the mound and across the coarse slick grass that had once been a lawn. "Lord, don't let me lose Thunder. He means so much to Lillian and Bill."

As she climbed the wide side steps, a dart of lightning zipped through the gray clouds piled on the horizon. Thunder crashed, making it sound like the old house was cracking into pieces around her—around the little white dog who bore the same name. She opened the door and stepped inside, her breath coming in ragged gasps.

The door slammed shut behind her and Marty's heart thudded against her ribs.

Chapter 17 / Trapped

Gradually Marty's eyes grew accustomed to the darkness. Odd shapes seemed to loom out at her.

The room was not so much furnished as it was full of furniture set here and there without order. Marty touched the back of a large ornamental chair with finely scrolled arms and crown emblems, noted the large pewter bowl sitting on top of the bureau alongside it.

Confusion gripped her. "What is this?" she murmured.

Her eye caught a flashing movement and the round white fluffball that was Thunder's tail disappeared through an open doorway leading into the depths of the house. She moved forward, threading her way through the furniture.

"Thunder!" she called.

Her voice echoed in the antiquated room, seeming to bounce off the wainscotting around the walls, the boards covering the windows. The silence that followed was oppressive.

Marty held her breath and listened. Slowly she became aware of a loud ticking sound. Goose bumps rose on her arms as she held her arms tightly against her body, trying to shrink inside herself. She spotted an old-fashioned grandfather clock close to her elbow, ticking away to itself, and drew a relieved breath.

She stepped through the open doorway where Thunder had disappeared. A stairway rose ahead and a faint light from an open door or window illuminated the stairwell, reflected in a gilded mirror gracing the wall.

Slowly she mounted the steps. A beautiful tapestry done in blues and pewter gray depicted a historical scene complete with knights in gleaming armor. Portraits, done in oils, looked down at her—one, a bearded man, another, a woman in a dark green dress with a plunging neckline. A flashing emerald necklace adorned her white throat.

The door at the bottom of the stairs creaked, then clicked ominously. Marty turned.

The door had closed. Her heart skipped a beat.

"Who's there?"

There was no reply. The bearded man questioned her presence. The emerald lady stared at her with enigmatic eyes—*like the Mona Lisa*.

Marty took a deep breath and tiptoed stealthily up the stairs.

This room was more as she'd imagined the whole house would be—spacious, devoid of furniture. But still there was no sign of a white fuzzy poodle with a wagging tail.

One of the wide boards nailed over the broken window was partially loose and Marty noticed broken panes of colored glass in the window corners. As she watched, the board swung open, letting in a blast of fresh air.

Marty ran to the window and looked out. She realized then she was at the front of the house, suspended in midair. Beneath her the pit yawned wide, a huge open-mouthed monster eager to swallow his prey.

A flash of lightning snaked earthwards and something heavy crashed against the house. Marty leaped backward.

The weather had gone crazy and she was alone in the middle of a world gone mad. Not even Thunder was with her. Another tremendous clap of thunder broke—a brilliant zigzaggy flash that flooded the surrounding countryside with eerie light.

Marty stood frozen. Would it be safest to go back downstairs or stay where she was? A footstep on the stairs decided for her. She turned and ran for the stairs above her.

No painting, mirrors or tapestries covered these walls. The stairs rose narrow and steep, plunging her into the middle of a small room. The roof sloped at each end so that the ceiling was only a few inches from the floor. Even in her fear she knew it must be the tower room.

She clapped her hand over her mouth to cut back a scream as a white catapult charged into her arms. "Oh, Thunder," she whispered, "why did you come up here?"

She hugged him close to her while his eager pink tongue dabbed at her cheeks, at her neck, even her hands. "Why, Thunder!" she exclaimed, "You're shaking!" She patted his silly white topknot and wondered at the slow dissolving of fear in the pit of her stomach.

The window facing the pit was wide open to the wind. It wildly rumpled Marty's hair and and parted Thunder's white fuzzy coat, showing the pink skin beneath.

"You're quite a dog, Thunder. You really are. But you'll have to be quiet. There's someone besides you and me in this house."

Thunder seemed to understand. He stilled his little paws and stopped his excited licking.

Marty looked around. The room was empty except for a large wooden crate and swath of black plastic. She set Thunder on the floor and clutched the crate with both hands, shoving and pushing it until it blocked the door.

"I hope whoever's in the house thinks it's only the storm making this racket," she murmured to the dog.

She sat back down and Thunder leaped into her lap. They listened together. The wind whistling around the tower drowned out other sounds. Her eyes examined the room, noting large scratches across the wooden floor.

Gradually the wild thumping of Marty's heart slowed. *Storm or no storm, I'm not going to let fear control me,* she thought. *I have a God who's bigger than the biggest storm. I need to trust His presence—His care.*

She eased her Bible out of her backpack without dislodging her fuzzy friend. She knew she'd read a verse in Psalms that talked about the elements out of control—her control—but not God's.

The verse jumped off the page, bringing tears to her eyes. She bent over the page and read it again: "In your distress you called and I rescued you, I answered you out of a thundercloud."

Slowly she turned the pages, a phrase here, a verse there: "His lightning lights up the world; the earth sees and trembles."

The thunder cracked, the wind screamed, and the floor trembled beneath her. "Lord," she whispered as she clutched Thunder's warm body, "I'm calling you in my distress. I need you to rescue me. Please answer me out of your thunderclouds."

Something hard slammed against the door. The crate barricading it moved toward her.

Thunder yipped and Marty reached down silencing him, her fingers curling around his muzzle. Fear wrapped itself around her as the door slowly opened.

"Steve!" Marty cried with relief.

He opened his arms and fell to his knees beside her on the wooden floor. Marty and Thunder were both in his arms.

"You're here," Marty whispered. "Did our God send you?"

She buried her face against his shoulder, blotting out the storm.

"Marty," Steve's voice was urgent, close to her ear. "Someone else is in the house."

Marty lifted her face. "What do you mean?"

"A man was watching. He followed you inside."

"Followed me? Then where is he now?" She shuddered. "Steve, this place is dangerous. Where were you that you saw all this?"

A flash of lightning lit the sky, making the room they sat in almost as bright as noonday. Steve looked at her searchingly.

"I had my tripod set up." He gestured in the opposite direction of the mound. "All of sudden Thunder came traipsing down the path with you following. The light was perfect just then—and Thunder ran through the door."

"And I followed."

Steve nodded. "Then I realized someone was hidden inside the upside-down tree. As soon as you disappeared through the door, he was on your trail."

Marty looked around apprehensively. "Perhaps he left?"

"I don't think so. When I slipped inside, I didn't see anyone. I started up the stairs, thinking that's where you might be when I heard the lock on the front door click."

They stared at each other.

"Marty," Steve said slowly, "we're locked inside this old fossil."

"Suspended over a gravel pit—in the middle of a raging storm."

"And you're not afraid," Steve marveled. "But then you needn't be. We can always break a window—knock out a board. Are you game to sneak downstairs, try to find out what this is all about?"

"The man—"

"There's two of us—one of him."

Marty jumped to her feet, holding Thunder beneath her arm. "What are we waiting for?"

Steve grabbed her hand and they stole softly through the open doorway leading to the stairs. Another thunderclap sounded, but this one was faintly muffled by the close walls.

They went down single file, Steve in the lead.

"The furniture downstairs," Marty said. "Did you see the clocks, the pewter bowl on the bureau?"

"Not the pewter bowl. But I saw the crystal one from the thrift store you described. The tulip design was unmistakable."

"Then we're on to something!" Marty exulted. "He—whoever 'he' is—is using this house as a place to store stolen antiques."

Steve and Marty stepped into the big open room as lightning stabbed the sky. The wind whacked the loose board against the windowsill. A low growl rumbled in Thunder's throat.

"Hush," Marty whispered. "It's only the wind."

But somehow the slamming sound made her fearful. Her fingers gripped Steve's hand tightly.

Once again they descended the stairway with the unusual wall hangings. "These are valuable," Steve whispered. "I'm sure they are."

Uncertainty made them hesitate on the threshold of the darkened room massed with furniture. It brooded around them and Marty shivered.

"There's no one here," Steve whispered. "Whoever it was must have left. Perhaps the storm—"

He let go of Marty's hand and dug into his pocket, removing the pocket light he carried. The tiny pinpoint of light highlighted the crystal bowl on top of the fireplace mantel. An old-fashioned doll with ruffled pink skirts leaned against the bowl.

Marty gasped and moved toward the fireplace.

At the same moment a loud crack charged the room with tension. Marty froze. The huge maple outside the house came down, slamming into the boarded window and spraying the room with broken glass. The light of early evening flooded the room. Another lightning flash and the great tree disappeared, plunging headlong into the pit. The earth shuddered beneath them.

"Let's get out of here!" Steve shouted.

"Not so fast," a voice behind them ordered.

They whirled.

Standing in front of the fireplace a stranger glared malevolently at them.

As the thunder clapped again, Marty stepped back into her past—her past that was part of her nightmares. She was a small girl again, standing in her parents' living room, clasping her Raggedy Ann close to her chest. There'd been a storm and she was frightened. She'd come out seeking reassurance . . .

"I know you!" Marty cried with the shock of remembering. "You were there—in my house—with my mother! Oh, it's not true! It can't be!"

Thunder growled and she buried her face in his topknot, shutting out the pain. The man strode toward her.

"I don't know what you're talking about," he said.

She looked up then and recognized the hard metallic eyes of the man who'd talked with Traci behind the camellia tree. Confusion gripped her. "Who are you?" she whispered. "Why do I feel that I know you—yet I *don't* know you?"

The man stopped abruptly as he recognized Marty. "Why, you're Lorraine's little girl!" He reached out and touched her honey-colored hair. "I should have known—your eyes, that hair—"

"You were there that night," Marty repeated in a hoarse whisper. Rain slashed through the open window, slashed at her own shattered emotions. "And I hate you. I—I was afraid of the storm. But when I came out . . . afraid . . . needing my mother, you . . . *you* were there with her."

The man stared at her incredulously. "You think—you mean you don't know?"

"I don't know what you're saying!" Marty cried. "I only know I've hated you for years—even though I buried that hate so deep. I tried to push it away because . . . because you stole my mother's love away from my father!"

Now she could understand why she felt so remote from her mother—the discomfort she'd felt when her father put his arm around her mother.

"You think your mother and I were . . . ?" He shook his head. "You mean Lorraine never told you who I was?"

Marty's lips quivered. "She never mentioned that night. And I—I couldn't. Somehow I blocked it out of my mind. But sometimes I'd dream." She shivered, remembering the nightmares, her fear of storms.

"I'm Lonnie," the man whispered, his voice low and heavy with regret. "She should have told you. I never meant to do it, Marty—never meant to pry you and your mother apart."

Steve entered the conversation for the first time. "Then maybe you need to explain. Marty doesn't know what you're saying, and I can't follow you either."

Lonnie turned to him. "I'm Lorraine's brother. Marty is my niece."

He looked at Marty. "I'm afraid I've destroyed something in your life, little girl. Something that may never be recaptured—your trust in your mother." He shook his head in bewilderment. "Lorraine was the only one who ever believed in me. Yet all I ever brought her was shame and pain.

"I'm sorry, Marty. I wanted to change. I tried. The night of the storm—the night you crept into the room hugging your doll—was the night I turned myself over to the law.

"I was in prison for almost eight years."

"And you go out to play the same role all over again?" Steve asked, his voice clipped and dry. He gestured around the room. "This room is full of stolen antiques."

The furrowed lines in Lonnie's forehead deepened. "I

didn't steal all of them. I found some of them stored in the tower room. I went up in the darkness, put up black plastic so no one would see, set up a floodlight."

"We saw the lights that night. You weren't as successful as you thought."

"The plastic slipped," Lonnie said bitterly. "I always fail. Not only did I fail Lorraine and Marty, I failed Traci too. She's my daughter. I never married her mother but she's mine nonetheless. I didn't want her to be involved in this, but she is."

Marty gasped. "Then it was she we saw that day in the red convertible. She must have been wearing a wig!"

Lonnie didn't seem to be listening. "Traci was tired of poverty—of scrimping and going without," he continued. "Antiques offered a steady cash flow. . . ."

He ran his hands through his hair. The thunderous storm was still raging outside, but no one seemed to notice anymore. "I'd made connections in prison and Traci had a friend who worked at the thrift store and her mother was there. She knew, too, this place was off limits, that it was safe—until you two started skulking around, that is.

"God knows I didn't want to do it, but I did it anyway. I tried to talk to Lorraine. She's my sister—I've always loved her, but she wouldn't let me back into her life. I don't blame her. She was only trying to protect her husband, her child—"

Thunder cracked across the sky, drowning out his voice.

"I'd made the early years of her marriage unbearable!" he shouted. "Put a wedge between her and Bob. He finally asked me to stop coming around, told me I was putting a tremendous strain on her emotions, ripping their marriage apart."

His words were cut short by a shuddering sound. The floor beneath them quaked and Lonnie's metallic eyes burned into theirs.

"Get out!" he cried. "The house is going into the pit!"

He rushed for the exit door. Time seemed to stand still as he wrestled with the lock. Then he had Marty by the shoulders.

"Run!" he shouted. "I'm going to save what I can." He shoved Marty ahead of him, onto the porch.

Marty ducked her head. She clung to Thunder with both hands and ran across the slickened boards, down the steps and into the storm. Within seconds she was soaked to the skin.

She slowed.

"Don't stop!" Steve shouted behind her. His hands touched her back, steering her toward the upside-down tree. Together they slid and slithered and clawed their way up the bank.

They stopped beneath the tree's sheltering branches and looked back. The earth beneath the house gave way slowly. The overhanging porch slanted downwards. The old house seemed to take a long, slow step forward, then go down with gracious, dignified majesty.

Its mighty crash trembled the branches of the upside-down tree and echoed inside Marty's heart. She hugged Thunder, seeking comfort, knowing the wetness on her cheeks was more than rain.

Steve knew it too. His arms came around her and Thunder, drawing them both close.

Chapter 18 / Lonnie's Choice

Marty stood in the living room, holding the wet bedraggled poodle in her arms. She hesitated uncertainly, her tennis shoes making ugly wet spots on the carpet. She shifted Thunder beneath her left arm and bent forward, fumbling with her wet laces, discarding soggy socks and shoes in a muddy pile.

"First off a warm bath for you, my shivering friend," she said as she walked barefoot to the bathroom.

"I don't know where Mom and Dad are," she added as she turned on the water with one hand. Gently she soaped the mud from Thunder's curly hair, then wrapped him in a thick brown towel.

She left her mud-encrusted jeans in a heap and ran up the stairs. Depositing Thunder in the middle of her bed, she headed for the shower, her robe dangling from her arm.

The warm water coupled with shampoo and creme rinse revived her. Afterward she sat on the edge of the bed and combed the tangles out of her hair while Thunder watched, gradually warming in his brown cocoon.

Footsteps neared her room and her mother rushed in without knocking. "Marty!" she cried. "The storm—" she spotted Thunder curled inside the towel. "You're both here. Lillian and I have been so worried."

"Where were you when I came in?" Marty asked.

"Lillian called. She got your note so I went over." She picked up Marty's phone and began dialing. "I'll call her, tell her you're both okay."

She spoke a few words, then replaced the receiver. "Dad called, said he was in the middle of a plumber's nightmare and wouldn't be home 'till late. What happened, Marty?" she asked. "You look done in."

Marty's lips quivered. "Thunder and I were caught in the storm. And—and—" She covered her face with her hands. "Oh, Mother," she wailed, "everything's so awful— and wonderful—all at the same time."

Her mother sat down on the bed and put her arms around her. The warmth and caring of her arms tore down the giant wall Marty had erected around her heart so long ago. Great wrenching sobs broke from deep inside her.

With compassionate insight, her mother held back her many questions, realizing that Marty needed the release of tears and the comfort of her love.

After awhile Marty sat up and fumbled for the tissues on the stand. "I don't know why I'm bawling like this," she whispered, wiping her eyes.

Moistness glinted in her mother's brown eyes. "You haven't cried in my arms since you were a little girl," she said softly, unsteadily. "I—Marty, I don't know how to say this, but it meant a lot to me."

Marty smiled tremulously. "I think I understand." She reached for another tissue and blew her nose furiously. "Mother, I need to tell you about tonight—the storm, Steve, my uncle, your brother Lonnie—"

"Lonnie!" her mother echoed.

Marty read apprehension in her dark eyes, in the sudden tenseness of her shoulders. She touched her mother's hand. "Let me tell it from the beginning."

The story came out in jumbled pieces, the rising storm

with Thunder running into the old house, the discovery of its ticking clocks and ancient bureaus, her fears as she climbed the steep stairs searching for Thunder.

"But you found him," her mother said soothingly. She touched the white ruff of hair on Thunder's head. "Poor dog."

"Oh, he was having fun," Marty protested. "At least he was until we started hearing noises. Then Steve came. He said he'd seen someone follow me inside. After a while we decided to go downstairs and look. That's when we saw Lonnie."

"Lonnie," her mother whispered. "My brother—my happy-go-lucky, shiftless brother." She leaned forward. "Marty, you've got to understand. Lonnie almost plunged your father and me into disaster, not only financially but emotionally as well.

"Your dad and Lonnie are opposites of each other. Bob is so hard working, so honest and steady. My brother— shiftless, dishonest, out to make a fast buck, trying to get what he could no matter whom he hurt."

Her knuckles whitened on her lap. "That time he hurt Bob. And Bob didn't want to fight back, didn't want to alienate him further. But he did, because he had too. He told Lonnie either to change—or get out of our lives.

"And I . . . I loved them both—my husband and my brother."

Marty swallowed, trying to rid herself of the lump forming inside her throat. "He loved you too," she whispered. "He said he did."

"Did he tell about the years in prison? How he came back into my life several weeks ago? Wanted me to give him another chance? I couldn't do it, Marty. I knew what kind of man he was and I'd promised your father. I couldn't jeopardize our relationship."

Her fingers twisted in her lap. "Besides, I didn't want

Lonnie back. Your father's and my relationship was too hard earned to risk again. And I knew Lonnie hadn't changed—except to get older, harder."

Marty nodded. "He'd stolen the antiques that were inside the house. But, Mother, I have to tell you something—something awful."

She clasped her own hands in her lap, clasped them until her knuckles turned white. "After Lonnie came, told us who he was, what he'd been doing, I found out something about me."

As she described the fears she'd bottled up inside her for so long—the nightmares—pain welled up inside her mother's eyes. "But I didn't know 'til tonight that they were based on something which happened long ago. Something I'd seen.

"I . . . I . . . the night Lonnie was with you—before he went to prison—I remembered stumbling into the room, scared because of the storm. I felt the emotions, but I misunderstood. I thought you were giving your love to another man besides Daddy." Her voice lowered to a whisper. "And I hated you for it. I think that's why I blocked it out. The pain was too great. I thought—"

Her mother made a soft moaning sound. "Oh, Marty, Marty, I never dreamed. You were so little! And I was only trying to protect you. I didn't want you to know my brother—your own uncle—was in prison! I didn't think you needed to know. That's why I never talked about it. And I had such mixed feelings—shame, love—"

"I know." Marty jumped to her feet. "Fear builds walls around one's emotions. It keeps one from accepting love—real love."

Her mother looked up at her. A half smile quirked her lips. "Marty, you're growing up," she said softly.

"I don't know. But I think I'm changing." Marty pointed to the picture of the house standing on the rock. "It started when I gave my heart to God. But it wasn't until tonight—

"Mother, the house on the cliff is gone. It fell into the pit. And, Mother, Lonnie—Lonnie went down with it."

Her mother crumbled before her eyes. Her face whitened, her chin trembled.

Marty put her arms around her. "Steve called the police and I came home. But before I did, I saw the rubble at the bottom of the pit."

She was silent, remembering the rain, the flashing lights of the police car, the ambulance, the men's running feet. "They said he didn't have a chance. But, Mother, there's something you need to know. Lonnie warned us the house was going down, shoved Steve and me out the door. He chose to go back inside to save what he could. But first he wanted to be sure his sister's kid made it to safety."

Her mother nodded. "He made a choice. I have to accept that."

She leaned back on the bed, propping herself up on her elbows. Thunder nuzzled her hair but she paid no attention and Marty didn't know what to say. Her mother seemed lost in thought, staring at the photo display.

Marty thought she was examining the details of Oregon grape and vine maples until she said, "The wise man and the foolish man made choices too. One chose to build his life on the principles Jesus taught. The other—"

"Lonnie chose the sand," Marty agreed. "Mother, I wanted to tell you before, but somehow I couldn't. I asked Jesus Christ to take charge of my life. I'm building my life on a different foundation now—obedience to His Word."

Her mother didn't respond but remained caught away in her own private thoughts. After a while she hugged Marty and slipped out of the room.

She needs time, Marty thought. *Time to sort it all out . . . Time to put the pieces of her life back together again.*

Another thought stabbed her. *I need to put some pieces*

back together in my own life, too. I need to talk to Carey.

Marty reached for the telephone.

The crashing autumn storm blew away the days of dismal rain, replacing them with bright sunshine. The day of Uncle Lonnie's graveside service dawned blue and clear and Marty was glad. Frost crisped the air, gave an early morning starkness to the bare trees and tipped the evergreens with pearly white.

She rode with her parents to the cemetery and waited in the car for Steve to arrive. When he pulled up alongside, she was surprised to see his parents with him.

"We wanted to come," Mr. Lawford explained, as they walked together to the mound of fresh dark brown earth, "—not because we knew your uncle, but because we wanted you and your family to know you aren't alone."

Just doing what God wants them to do, Marty thought as she thanked them. Another car pulled up and Marty turned. Would it be Traci?

It wasn't. "Mr. Merwyn!" she gasped. She looked at Steve. "Did you know he was coming?"

Steve nodded. "He wanted you to know that's he's not holding anything against your family. In fact, he said—never mind. I'll let him tell you himself."

The old man with the salt-and-pepper beard, still wearing denim overalls, strode toward them, his hands behind his back. He stopped in front of Steve and Marty.

His gray eyes seemed to penetrate Marty's thoughts, lay bare her deepest feelings. "I'm sorry about your uncle," he said. "But I want you to know I'm not going to make trouble for anyone. Steve told me about my dollhouse being in the antique store in Astoria. The police talked to the owners. They're bringing it home."

He shifted from one foot to the other and lowered his eyes.

The twelve red roses he thrust into Marty's arms made

her gasp. "Oh, Mr. Merwyn!"

"They're not for him." He nodded toward the grave. "The flower in the car is. These are for you—your own personal flowers to cheer you up."

Marty's fingers touched the velvety rose petals. "Mr. Merwyn, thank you. They're beautiful. But you shouldn't have."

"You did something for my daughter and I guess I have a right to return the favor. But that's not the real reason. I like what you're letting God do in your life. You're all right."

He strode to his car and came back carrying a huge potted gold chrysanthemum in front of him. He set it beside the grave and stood with bowed head beside the casket.

The scene before Marty blurred. She looked down at the roses in her arms, then up at Steve.

The service was short, the words few. Afterward Steve's parents went home with Mr. Merwyn. Marty's mother and father came over and hugged her, then slipped away. Steve and Marty wandered through the graveyard.

"Traci hasn't been in school, but I really thought she might come to her father's burial," Marty said after a while.

Steve shook his head. "I went over to the store when she didn't come to class," he said. "According to her mother, few people knew Lonnie and Traci's relationship. Traci has rough days ahead of her."

"Yes," Marty agreed. "She was involved in burglary and that's heavy."

"A felony, I think. I wonder how it'll turn out."

Marty sighed. "It's sad somehow. My own cousin. But I never knew—never dreamed. And all this time I disliked her, almost hated her. I wish I knew how to let her know I care."

"You're a resourceful person," Steve said sensibly. "You'll find a way."

He grabbed her hand. "Marty, would you like to drive over to our special spot? I've something I want to show you there. Besides, I'd like to know what our cliff looks like now that the house is gone."

Marty nodded. "I'd like to see, too."

Before they left, she laid one of the red roses Mr. Merwyn had given her beside the fresh grave. "From me," she said softly. Then turning to Steve, murmured, "I'm ready now."

Marty and Steve stood close together beneath the spreading cedar tree and looked at the changed cliff face. The house lay tumbled into brokenness on the gravel-pit floor. The tower was crushed, the porch splintered.

"It's gone forever," Marty said softly. "Oh, Steve, it's sad, isn't it? And you never got a photo of it. There are only mine and they're not nearly as good as yours."

Steve grinned broadly. "Surprise." He slid a large flat envelope from beneath his jean jacket.

"I wanted to show you this while we were here." He thrust the folder into her hands. "Open it."

Marty drew out a photograph. Billowing white storm clouds caught her attention: the old house, the thrusting tower, the wide porch. "Thunder!"

Steve bent over her shoulder. "He was there, running across the porch, and you right behind. He adds something, doesn't he?"

"I guess! Steve, it's beautiful—the best you've done."

"I agree. It's too late to enter the contest, but it doesn't matter. Not anymore. Just taking it proved something to me. I know now I have what it takes to succeed as a photo journalist. It's something I long to do—will do."

"I know you will!" Marty exclaimed. "But, Steve, I have a surprise for you, too. I talked with Carey. She called the magazine, told them what she'd done. Then she told them about your ruined photos."

"Really? What did they say?"

"They complimented her on her honesty. Told her to encourage you to send yours in anyway, that they were always looking for superior photos to use in their magazine."

She looked at the photograph. "This photo is something else. They're sure to take it. Those clouds, brooding atmosphere." She put her finger on Thunder's ridiculously red-ribboned head. "Today meets yesterday."

Looking down, she toyed with the two red roses she'd tucked deep inside her wide jacket pocket. "Steve—"

"Speak to me, oh, lovely one," he encouraged. "What is it?"

She blushed. "It's silly but . . ." She held a rose out to him. "I brought these two—one for each of us—to always remind us to build our lives on a solid foundation, our Rock, the Lord Jesus Christ."

Steve took the rose. "You're not being silly," he whispered softly. "I don't want to ever forget this place. I want to be reminded to always choose His way. Marty, I love you."

Marty trembled with joy as he put his arm around her shoulders and gently kissed her.

"Oh, Steve, I love you too!"

He took her hand and they joyfully headed for home.